Advance Man

Part One of
The Honeycomb Trilogy

Mac Rogers

A SAMUEL FRENCH ACTING EDITION

SAMUEL
FRENCH
FOUNDED 1830

SAMUELFRENCH.COM
SAMUELFRENCH-LONDON.CO.UK

FOR PRODUCTION ENQUIRIES

UNITED STATES AND CANADA
Info@SamuelFrench.com
1-866-598-8449

UNITED KINGDOM AND EUROPE
Plays@SamuelFrench-London.co.uk
020-7255-4302

Each title is subject to availability from Samuel French, depending upon country of performance. Please be aware that *ADVANCE MAN* may not be licensed by Samuel French in your territory. Professional and amateur producers should contact the nearest Samuel French office or licensing partner to verify availability.

MUSIC USE NOTE

Licensees are solely responsible for obtaining formal written permission from copyright owners to use copyrighted music in the performance of this play and are strongly cautioned to do so. If no such permission is obtained by the licensee, then the licensee must use only original music that the licensee owns and controls. Licensees are solely responsible and liable for all music clearances and shall indemnify the copyright owners of the play(s) and their licensing agent, Samuel French, against any costs, expenses, losses and liabilities arising from the use of music by licensees. Please contact the appropriate music licensing authority in your territory for the rights to any incidental music.

IMPORTANT BILLING AND CREDIT REQUIREMENTS

If you have obtained performance rights to this title, please refer to your licensing agreement for important billing and credit requirements.

THE HONEYCOMB TRILOGY was originally presented by Gideon Productions in three separate productions over the first half of 2012 at The Secret Theatre in Long Island City, New York. *ADVANCE MAN* ran in January 2012, *BLAST RADIUS* in March and April 2012, and *SOVEREIGN* in June 2012. The performances were directed by Jordana Williams, produced by Sean Willams and Shaun Bennet Fauntleroy, with sets by Sandy Yaklin, costumes by Amanda Jenks, lights by Sarah Lurie, sound by Jeanne Travis, props and effects by Stephanie Cox-Williams, fight choreography by Joseph Mathers, alien leg design by Zoe Morsotte, and publicity by Emily Owens PR. The Production Stage Manager was Devan Hibbard. The cast was as follows:

BILL	Sean Williams
AMELIA	Kristen Vaughan
RONNIE	Becky Byers
ABBIE	David Rosenblatt
CONOR	Jason Howard
VALERIE	Shaun Bennet Fauntleroy
BELINDA	Rebecca Comtois
RAF	Abraham Makany
LYNN	Amanda Duarte
KIP	Brian Silliman

THE HONEYCOMB TRILOGY was subsequently presented by Gideon Productions in repertory at the Gym At Judson in New York City in October and November of 2015. The performances were directed by Jordana Williams and produced by Sean Williams, Rebecca Comtois, and Mikell Kober, with sets by Sandy Yaklin, costumes by Amanda Jenks, lights by Jennifer Wilcox, sound by Jeanne Travis, blood effects by Stephanie Cox-Williams, alien leg design by Zoe Morsotte and Lauren Genutis, fight choreography by Adam Swiderski, and publicity by Emily Owens PR. The Production Stage Manager was Viki Barclay and the Assistant Director was Sara Thigpen.

BILL	Sean Williams
AMELIA	Kristen Vaughan
RONNIE	Becky Byers
ABBIE	David Rosenblatt
CONOR	Jason Howard
VALERIE	Shaun Bennet Fauntleroy
BELINDA	Rebecca Comtois
RAF	Carlos Martin
LYNN	Ana Maria Jomolca
KIP	Brian Silliman

CHARACTERS

The Cooke family members can be any race/ethnicity. It would probably work best if they look biologically related.

BILL COOKE – 40s, male
AMELIA COOKE – 40s, female
RONNIE COOKE – 18, female
ABBIE COOKE – 15, male
CONOR – 40s, male, any ethnicity
VALERIE – 40s, female, any ethnicity
BELINDA – 30s, female, any ethnicity
RAF – 30s, male, Latino
KIP – 40s to 60s, any ethnicity
LYNN – 30s to 50s, any ethnicity

SETTING

Coral Gables, Florida, a few years in the future. The play takes place in the Cooke family's living room.

ACT ONE

One

(The living room of the Cooke home, an upper-middle-class house in Coral Gables, Florida. A front door leading outside is visible, as is another leading to the kitchen. A staircase leads upstairs.)

(LYNN watches AMELIA COOKE minister to a distressed man, CONOR.)

AMELIA. All right, now sshh, sshh, Conor, you're all right. You're okay. Right?

CONOR. Meel-ee-yah.

AMELIA. That's right, Conor! That's so good!

CONOR. Eh-mee-lee-yah.

AMELIA. That's just so good. Now, Conor, are you on me? Are you watching me?

CONOR. Mee-lee-yah.

(AMELIA stands a little away from CONOR and holds her hands out.)

AMELIA. That's right, now walk to me, Conor. Walk to me.

(He does, slowly, then holds on to her. She moves away again.)

Now again, Conor, walk to me. (*to* LYNN, *as he does*) The ritual, it…

LYNN. Sure.

(CONOR walks to AMELIA.)

AMELIA. Now Conor, when I say "When is dinner?" When I say "When is dinner?"

CONOR. 'N is dinner?

AMELIA. What do you say?

CONOR. "D'ner esss soon."

> (**LYNN** *picks up a few college brochures on the table, studies them.*)

AMELIA. When is dinner?

CONOR. D'ner iss soon.

AMELIA. Conor, when is dinner?

CONOR. When is dinner, dinner is soon.

> (*They are now in an upstage corner.*)

AMELIA. That's perfect, Conor. I'm so proud of you.

> (*She returns to* **LYNN**.)

He'll stay there. That's his spot.

LYNN. That's fine.

AMELIA. Of course eight years ago he would have made anyone's shortlist of the ten best astronauts in the world.

> (*Beat.* **LYNN** *holds up a college brochure.*)

LYNN. Veronica.

AMELIA. My daughter – we call her Ronnie – who just –

LYNN. The one with blood on her clothes.

AMELIA. I'm sorry you had to see that.

LYNN. Good school.

AMELIA. (*reflexively cleaning up the brochures*) Well, we'll see what happens.

LYNN. Because we'd talked about meeting alone…

AMELIA. I wasn't expecting – I got a call from their assistant principal to pick them up.

LYNN. Both of them?

AMELIA. And then of course anything unpredictable puts Conor in a tailspin, and if it involves Abbie being upset you can double that.

LYNN. So Abbie's your son, Ronnie's your daughter, and I'm…your friend from college.

AMELIA. Thank you for going along with that.

LYNN. Reflex in my line of work. If she'd started asking questions, though…

AMELIA. Well, fortunately, her need to affect utter boredom about anything concerning me worked to our advantage. *(meaning* **CONOR***)* Is it all right that he's here?

LYNN. He can't understand us, right? Or repeat what we say to your husband? Unless he's recovering faster than reports suggest.

AMELIA. *(taking that in)* You're…remarkably prepared.

LYNN. A case like this, I don't have to prepare. I already read the news every day.

AMELIA. I don't know how we start this conversation.

LYNN. I got the basic idea from the email. Pretty standard, it's the job I do the most. Now how sure are you it's one of the other astronauts?

AMELIA. God, I hate this.

LYNN. Of course.

AMELIA. I might call this off. I can pay you for coming out here. How much would that be?

LYNN. Of course you hate this. This type of job, every time, woman or man, they always say, "I can't believe I'm doing this, I'm a cliché, I thought I'd have some dignity."

AMELIA. Yes! Exactly!

LYNN. I always say: "Why should you have dignity? Seriously. This is the most important thing in your life, the foundation of your adult life. If you still had dignity it would mean you didn't actually care." *(beat)*

AMELIA. If I'm right – *if* I'm right – it's one of the crew of the *Celeste Farrow*.

LYNN. And we're sure – and it'll help me if you're honest – we're fairly sure it's a woman.

AMELIA. Would be. If it's true.

LYNN. Guys can hide it for decades.

AMELIA. You have to know Bill. He could be gay; he could never be closeted.

LYNN. That squares. So: five astronauts with Bill on the *Celeste*. Tom Wiley, died on Mars, Conor Wells *(gesturing at* **CONOR***)*, Raf Nevares, and our two suspects: Valerie Tindal and Belinda Phifer.

AMELIA. Oh my god, "suspects."

LYNN. And you and Bill have been married...

AMELIA. Nineteen years.

LYNN. And you've never been concerned before now?

AMELIA. No, I, no.

LYNN. Why not?

AMELIA. It's not just that the, the intimacy had continued to – Jesus, I'm being ridiculous – We still had sex. On a regular, on what seemed to me to be an admirable basis.

LYNN. No dry spells.

AMELIA. Well, the three years he was flying to Mars and back.

LYNN. Sure.

AMELIA. And a bit after he came back.

LYNN. Because of Tom Wiley, because of... *(indicating* **CONOR***)*

AMELIA. I'm doing this wrong, I'm sitting here talking about the sex, and I'm completely talking around the real thing.

LYNN. The attention. *(beat)* It's the job I do the most.

AMELIA. All right, the attention, but Bill takes it to another level. When he turns it on you... Everyone else I know is sort of listening and sort of thinking about what they need to do later. You're doing it now, I'm sorry, just to illustrate the point.

LYNN. But not Bill.

AMELIA. For Bill, there's his family, and there's the crew of the *Celeste*. He doesn't give away his attention – or his heart – easily, but when he does it's absolute. *(meaning* **CONOR***)* Why do you think he's here? He should be in a hospital, of course he should be in a hospital, but he served on the *Celeste*, so he's Bill's brother.

LYNN. So if he's having an affair:

AMELIA. Then he's having an *affair*, with feelings and the whole catastrophe. It's possible that you think I'm naïve.

LYNN. Nah. Client instincts are usually pretty good on these jobs. Anyway, it's the best place to start. So, Valerie Tindal and Belinda Phifer. You like one more than the other?

AMELIA. Like meaning "suspect"?

LYNN. Sorry, yeah.

AMELIA. Well, that's the problem. He spent two years of training, three years in flight, and now works far into the evening with both of them.

LYNN. He works late every night?

AMELIA. Which doesn't necessarily mean anything. Chinampas is a huge project, farms to oversee all over the world, and they won't bring in extra staff.

LYNN. *(checking notes)* The... "Chinampas Terraform Initiative." This feed-the-world-with-swamp-vegetables thing that they quit being astronauts for. "Chinampas..."

AMELIA. Originally a method of swamp-farming favored by the Aztecs.

LYNN. I had a chance to look over a couple interviews he did about it. He's outspoken.

AMELIA. Certainly my husband's political views have earned him more enemies than friends. Do you have something you want to say about it?

LYNN. Hey, a job's a job. Nobody pays me to have opinions. All I'm saying is it's possible that your husband has more than one reason right now to be distracted and less frisky in the bedroom, right?

AMELIA. No one pays you for opinions, but they do pay you to speculate?

LYNN. Well, until you pay me my day rate to follow your husband around, speculate is all I can do.

AMELIA. I'd like to pay your day rate to follow my husband around.

LYNN. I'll get you an invoice. The email's private, right?

AMELIA. I created it for this purpose.

LYNN. And generally speaking, when they're not flying to farms or speaking engagements, they're at the Chinampas offices?

AMELIA. Nearly always.

LYNN. Then it's time to buy some snacks and start sitting in my car.

AMELIA. Or – I don't know if this is helpful or – they will all be here Saturday.

LYNN. Here at this house?

AMELIA. Primarily in this room, I expect.

LYNN. What's the occasion?

AMELIA. We're having a dinner party for one of the investors.

LYNN. The whole crew's gonna be here?

AMELIA. There's dinner with Mr. Jackson – that's the investor – and then after he leaves the drinking and the war stories begin. Bill's already said that I'm welcome to stay up with them, of course, but I'll probably be bored, not knowing the references.

LYNN. Code for: put the kids to bed and let me and the boys watch the game.

AMELIA. As you say.

LYNN. You know what I could do.

AMELIA. I'm sorry?

LYNN. I could wire it up.

AMELIA. Wire what up?

LYNN. This room. I could wire it up and record the whole night.

AMELIA. Everything they say in this room.

LYNN. I mean, it'll be a big group hang, they won't be alone, so we may not get anything, but it's easier than wiring a secured office. It's a start.

AMELIA. What would you need to do?

LYNN. Come back with my gear. Some time when it's just you here, no kids. Barring another call from the assistant principal, I guess.

AMELIA. I'm sorry about that.

LYNN. Couldn't care less.

AMELIA. About the blood on Ronnie's shirt –

LYNN. Someone was picking on Abbie and Ronnie gave them a bloody nose.

AMELIA. How could you possibly know that?

LYNN. Abbie looks like the type of kid who gets hurt so easily it makes other kids wanna hurt him more. And Ronnie's got a temper. And they called you to pick up *both* of them. It doesn't take Sherlock Holmes.

AMELIA. Abbie's like his father: He's brilliant and he feels everything in the world. Ronnie's like her father: She's so angry and she never backs down.

LYNN. They must take after you a little bit.

AMELIA. No. Send me the invoice. I'll email you back with a time.

Two

(Later that night. **BILL** *and* **AMELIA** *are in the living room.)*

BILL. So, okay, just let me understand:

AMELIA. Bill, look –

BILL. Our son has, for months now, been the target of a pack of teenage shitheads, a pack of fucking vicious, homophobic animals who –

AMELIA. You know what, don't even bring that into it.

BILL. Why not? We know that's part of it.

AMELIA. And can we please not decide our son's sexuality before he decides it for himself?

BILL. We know when our daughter caught them in the act, she didn't hesitate before walking –

AMELIA. What I'm talking about is what we want Ronnie to –

BILL. Walking right into harm's way and punching their ringleader in the fucking face –

AMELIA. "In harm's way," for God's sake –

BILL. Which brings us to now, when we are somehow *not* taking them out for pizza and beer.

AMELIA. What I'm saying is: what do we want Ronnie to take away from this?

BILL. Besides a medal?

AMELIA. That's what you want? That when faced with a challenging situation, your advice to her, as her father, is that she should start throwing punches?

BILL. Jesus Christ, Milly –

AMELIA. What do you want her to take away –

BILL. I say, "Our daughter stood up for our son, and that's commendable," and you say I'm condemning her to a life of fistfights in alleys!

*(**CONOR** appears at the top of the stairs. He descends slowly over the following.)*

AMELIA. How is saying "That's commendable" any different from saying, "You made the right choice today, so in a similar situation tomorrow, you should do the same thing"?

BILL. How is not reacting to bullies any different from telling them they can keep on doing –

AMELIA. You're saying "reacting" as a way to avoid saying "punching" –

BILL. Can I get to the end of a sentence?

AMELIA. Conor. *(beat)*

BILL. Hey bud. What's up? How are you there, bud? You can come on down. Come on down. Look at you walking! Look at you, that is some fine walking. That is some advance-level walking, bud, look at you.

(**CONOR** *gets all the way to* **BILL.**)

CONOR. Bill.

BILL. You see? A genius. People ask me about you all day long, and I say, "Conor's a genius." Now her. Now do her.

AMELIA. Bill, he's really tired, you shouldn't –

CONOR. Eh-mee-lee-yah.

BILL. Yeah, bud, that's right! That's absolutely right!

AMELIA. That was lovely, Conor.

(**CONOR** *goes to his corner.*)

BILL. I mean…

AMELIA. We have to tell her something.

BILL. Why? Why don't we just talk to her? Why don't we just have a conversation?

AMELIA. Because we're not her pals, we're her mom and dad. I'd love to have a conversation with Ronnie, you think I wouldn't love that? But she's our teenage daughter, that won't happen again for a decade. Right now we have to tell her something.

BILL. Ah, shit. (**BILL** *goes to the stairs.*) Ronnie? Ronnie!

AMELIA. Bill. She can't hear you from her room. How long have you lived here?

BILL. Yeah, all right, I'm going.

>*(He starts up the stairs when **RONNIE** appears from where she was hiding – just out of sight at the top of the stairs.)*

RONNIE. Okay guys, seriously: in what world was I not listening in on everything you guys said?

AMELIA. Ronnie, come downstairs, please.

BILL. So you were what, you were lurking?

RONNIE. You think I'd walk into this unprepared?

BILL. Fair enough.

AMELIA. Ronnie, come downstairs and have a seat, please.

RONNIE. See the thing is, Mom, I would? But it doesn't seem like there's a united front yet. And while you guys are busy getting your shit together, my brother's hungry and he's too scared to come downstairs. So I'm thinkin', maybe I'll grab a box of cereal or whatever and you guys can call me when you get on the same page?

AMELIA. You know what?

BILL. I actually brought home some sandwiches –

AMELIA. Sometimes you're just a jerk. It's not that you're an adolescent or you're smarter than your peers or you're trying on identities or any of it. Sometimes you're just a jerk.

RONNIE. That's right. Work off your guilt on me. I won't cry, unlike my *hungry brother.*

AMELIA. All right, that is *it*, if you're not able to act in a –

BILL. *(overlapping)* Why don't we – Milly – Milly – there's sandwiches, actually, I was thinking, there's a silver bag in the fridge, it's like four or five sandwiches, we ordered in today, we ordered too many, so in the silver bag, if you look in the fridge, I brought some home, you can't miss it, it's the totally out of place silver bag.

AMELIA. You want me to bring you *sandwiches*?

BILL. Not *me*, I'm saying –

RONNIE. *Abbie*. He wants you to feed Abbie. He wants you to feed dinner to your son.

BILL. Oh Ronnie, shut up.

AMELIA. So, I leave, and you two just sort it out.

BILL. Look, we're all tired, we're all –

AMELIA. You just have a quick, quiet talk and you sort it all out.

BILL. It's just, we're all wrung out, so…

> *(Beat.* **AMELIA** *leaves to the kitchen.)*

It's just, it's there, it's a silver bag, if you look in the fridge, you should just be able to…

> *(***AMELIA*** *re-enters with a silver bag and walks past them and up the stairs and exits.)*

RONNIE. *(calling after* **AMELIA***)* Don't like get a plate or a napkin or anything.

BILL. Do you know how to knock somebody out?

RONNIE. You wanna know what everybody's missing here?

BILL. I don't care. Do you know –

RONNIE. It's all the times I saw it and I *didn't* do anything. That's what's hilarious. You're all focused on today, and nobody gives a shit about all those times I saw them shoving him, and I did nothing. Somehow I'm not being punished for *that*. Somehow it's all about –

BILL. *Do you know.* How to knock a person unconscious?

RONNIE. Um…

BILL. You want the brain to hit the side of the skull, so you need their head to snap to one side fast. So generally the jaw punch is what you're looking for. Do what I do.

RONNIE. For real?

BILL. So, left leg forward, knees bent – c'mon, are we doing this or not? Left leg forward, knees bent…

RONNIE. Okay…

BILL. Right arm starting at the side, twist at the waist, aim for the jaw, just the jaw…and as you go, tighten up your body into the twist. You're not punching with your fist, you're punching with your whole body.

> *(They punch together.)*

RONNIE. Okay, is class dismissed or whatever?

BILL. Now you by yourself.

RONNIE. Can I just please sit through the lecture and go to –

BILL. Now you by yourself.

> **(RONNIE** *punches, then looks at* **BILL** *with a "Happy now?" shrug.)*

Number one: if you disrespect your mother again I will actually, I swear to God, spank you. I will actually do that, I will actually resurrect that, I will spank you. Right? *(beat)*

RONNIE. *(quieter)* And now, like, what, a lecture on "Violence doesn't solve anything"?

BILL. Well…okay.

RONNIE. What?

BILL. Here's the thing. Let's say you're an adult, you're an adult in the world we have now.

RONNIE. Oh, what, this is, like a –

BILL. Yeah, this is a hypothetical.

RONNIE. What's "the world we have now"?

BILL. You're an adult in the world we have now. Somebody hurts you, or humiliates you –

RONNIE. "If standing up for the people who cannot stand up for themselves is not the noblest pursuit of humankind, then nobility has no meaning."

BILL. Okay, seriously?

RONNIE. Celebrated astronaut William Cooke.

BILL. Did you seriously Google my speeches so you could come down here with some half-assed piece of ammo like that?

RONNIE. Did you mean it or was it just something –

BILL. I've walked on another planet, how easily impressed do you think I am? Somebody hurts you in the world we have now. And you see their face, and they're sneering, and they're so happy about how they hurt you, and you have two choices: you back down, they go off laughing, you carry the humiliation with you, you fantasize about revenge – which makes the humiliation worse – but then time goes by, and you think about it less and less until you hardly ever think about it again.

RONNIE. Okay, I get it –

BILL. Or, you clock him in his laughing face, and then when he's startled, keep hitting him until he doesn't laugh again for a long time. Now all of a sudden you've got police, you've got a guy and his friends out there thinking about revenge, and more than any of that, you've got a habit. And that makes it easier to do it again the next time, and the time after that, even though each time the consequences get worse: police, courts, criminal records, enemies looking for revenge. What I'm saying –

RONNIE. Dad, I *got* it, I got it like several sentences ago –

BILL. *What I'm saying is*, you want a united front? Here it is: your mom's right. In the world we have now, back down.

RONNIE. Why do you keep saying –

BILL. But if the world *changed* – and this is the only place where your mom and I differ – if the world changed, and the things that are in place now aren't in place anymore… I just wouldn't want you to forget how to use that right arm. *(beat)*

RONNIE. All right.

BILL. Well, then, yeah. We should eat something.

RONNIE. Dad, Abbie's gonna come down in a minute.

BILL. Sure.

RONNIE. Or in an hour or…whenever.

BILL. Or I can go up, if that's –

RONNIE. Is it possible to…not even bring it up? Like, at all? I'm not saying *ever*, just not tonight. *(beat)*

BILL. You're my favorite. Of my two children.

RONNIE. Okay you are so full of shit –

BILL. Other parents say, "I could never choose between my children," but I just say "Ronnie."

RONNIE. You completely don't, that never happens.

BILL. Do you think they ate all the sandwiches…? *(turns toward the stairs, sees **ABBIE**)*

ABBIE. *(terrified)* Dad?

BILL. I haven't seen anything on "The Honeycomb" for I think a week, is that possible?

ABBIE. Um…

BILL. Actually, I've been coming home pretty late, I think it's been two weeks, right?

ABBIE. I do have some new stuff.

BILL. Well where is it?

ABBIE. Just a second! *(He runs up the stairs and exits.)*

BILL. Sandwiches – Abbie – sandwiches!

RONNIE. They're gonna kick me out of school.

BILL. Well, except that your dad's a famous astronaut who's going to pull strings unavailable to other students.

RONNIE. You can joke about it, but it actually isn't fair.

BILL. Well, maybe there's a time coming when things will be fair, but until it does, I'm gonna revel in the unfairness just a little longer.

> *(**ABBIE** comes running down the stairs with several drawings.)*

ABBIE. This is everything I've done for two weeks.

BILL. Hand it over.

> *(As **BILL** takes the drawings and looks through them, **RONNIE** scoots over next to him to look. **ABBIE** goes to **CONOR**.)*

ABBIE. Conor? I wanna say… I'm really sorry I scared you. I was really upset when I came in, and I didn't think how it would…

CONOR. Abbie.

> *(It's quiet and tender and* **BILL** *and* **RONNIE** *don't hear.)*

RONNIE. *(studying the drawings)* So are they like monks?

BILL. They do look like monks.

ABBIE. That's what I was thinking. They live together on one big monastery on their planet and they each have their own cell they pray in and if you looked at all the cells from above –

BILL. *(holding one drawing up)* Oh yeah.

ABBIE. Yeah, where if you looked at it from above it would look like a honeycomb.

BILL. You know, you don't have to call it "Honeycomb," that's just a suggestion –

ABBIE. No, it's perfect.

> *(***AMELIA*** *comes part-way down the stairs with the sandwiches.)*

RONNIE. So…they're monks…with three eyes.

ABBIE. *(going to the couch)* I don't know, that's just what I'm trying.

RONNIE. Where are the balloons?

ABBIE. Balloons?

RONNIE. Don't people usually talk in comics?

ABBIE. Oh, I'm so not there yet. I don't know what anybody even looks like.

BILL. Have you thought about insects?

ABBIE. Is that too crazy? I was thinking about that.

BILL. Well, who lives in a honeycomb?

ABBIE. I guess.

BILL. You know what? Look at hive minds, look up um… can you reach my phone…?

RONNIE. *(getting the smartphone)* You guys are like, whatever's *beyond* nerds.

BILL. Look up eusocial behavior, look up... *(speaks into phone)* Look up swarm intelligence. Okay, yeah, now we're onto something.

> (**AMELIA** *watches the rest of her family gathered around* **BILL**'s *phone.*)

Three

(Night. ABBIE is at the living room table, drawing on a pad. There are papers scattered everywhere with drawings of strange insects on them. CONOR watches ABBIE draw. RONNIE enters over the following.)

ABBIE. Okay…just a sec…and…

(He shows the drawing to CONOR.)

Yeah?

(CONOR reacts positively.)

CONOR. Abbie.

ABBIE. Better?

CONOR. Abbie. Abbie.

ABBIE. Yeah, yeah, I know, I'm gonna do that part, I just haven't done it yet. But this is okay?

CONOR. Dinner is soon.

ABBIE. Okay then. Let me do it.

RONNIE. Abbie what the hell, why are you up?

ABBIE. You're late.

RONNIE. Are Mom and Dad up?

ABBIE. You are so deeply late.

RONNIE. I'm not *late*. I wasn't supposed to be out of the house at all.

ABBIE. So you're like, what…

RONNIE. I'm AWOL.

ABBIE. Shut up.

RONNIE. I'm so totally AWOL.

ABBIE. Were you out getting fingerblasted?

RONNIE. What?

ABBIE. Is there a guy, right now, in like his early twenties, driving back to his dorm room getting the secretions from your vagina all over his steering wheel?

RONNIE. Oh my god!

ABBIE. What, now you're shocked?

RONNIE. I'm so shocked!

ABBIE. Shocked and fingerblasted. Fingerblasted and shocked.

RONNIE. Look at you, you're so proud of your new word.

ABBIE. You didn't answer the question.

RONNIE. The answer's no.

ABBIE. Really?

> *(She sits next to **ABBIE** and starts paging through his drawings.)*

RONNIE. He totally washed his hands. He's more into the car than me.

ABBIE. Okay.

RONNIE. Aw, did I ruin your awesome burn? It was a good burn, Abbie. I'm crying all the tears.

ABBIE. Shut up.

RONNIE. If you came home from a date and I was like, "Haha you got a handjob" would you brood and cry forever?

ABBIE. Okay, no.

RONNIE. Getting finger-blasted is *good*, it feels *good*. If you're getting finger-blasted it means you're doing something right. I snuck out in the middle of the night, when I'm *already in trouble*, and I took that risk specifically so I could get finger-blasted.

ABBIE. Okay, I've now mega-absorbed your point.

RONNIE. *(rising to leave)* Go to sleep, dickhead. You can't get through school on nothing.

ABBIE. You didn't say anything.

RONNIE. About what?

ABBIE. About the new stuff.

RONNIE. Okay, so I didn't.

ABBIE. Well…say something.

RONNIE. Abbie, you can't do that.

ABBIE. Do what?

RONNIE. Just demand people say what they think of your stuff. If people wanna tell you, they'll tell you.

ABBIE. Why can't I just ask?

RONNIE. You're just basically begging people to lie to you.

ABBIE. Because it's bad?

RONNIE. Because they're not ready to say something. You have to let people come to you.

ABBIE. What about you? Can I just ask you?

RONNIE. Well, unfortunately, yeah.

ABBIE. So? The new characters, what do you think?

RONNIE. You mean the giant roaches?

ABBIE. They're not roaches.

RONNIE. Whatever they are.

ABBIE. Look at them! Do they look like roaches?

RONNIE. Hey! Guess who likes fingerblasting and isn't an entomologist?

ABBIE. So you don't like them.

RONNIE. I mean just like as drawings they're good, nobody else can draw giant roaches like you – or not roaches, fine – but like: this is supposed to be a comic, right?

ABBIE. So?

RONNIE. So, characters in comics have emotions and feelings, right?

ABBIE. What does that have to do with what –

RONNIE. So, where do I look on this not-a-roach guy to figure out what his emotions are?

ABBIE. But doesn't that make it better? That you have to work harder to guess?

RONNIE. It barely has a face!

ABBIE. So you look at body language, you watch its actions, you work it out! Faces are so fucking obvious, I'm so sick of faces!

RONNIE. I liked your faces.

ABBIE. You and everybody.

RONNIE. How you'd draw somebody and then they'd freak out, and be like, "Does he think I look like this? Wait *do* I look like this?"

ABBIE. But I'm not doing that anymore.

RONNIE. No, now you're doing...whatever this is.

ABBIE. A graphic novel.

RONNIE. And why?

ABBIE. Because this is the next thing.

RONNIE. Because it was Dad's idea.

ABBIE. Because this is the next step for me.

RONNIE. Because Dad's ideas are always awesome, and anything Dad suggests is totally the greatest. "You know what you should draw? A comic book called 'The Honeycomb'!"

ABBIE. "Honeycomb" was my idea.

RONNIE. No. It wasn't. Dad said it first. This is what he does. He puts ideas in your brain and makes you think they're yours.

ABBIE. Me?

RONNIE. Everybody.

ABBIE. So you're saying what, there's no way I could actually just care about this myself, I'm just Dad's puppet.

RONNIE. I just liked your faces, okay? I don't like this. I'm sorry. Oh Conor, honestly.

ABBIE. What?

(They both look at **CONOR**.*)*

RONNIE. It's like he's your dog. You get upset, it's like you can see the hairs on his back stand up.

ABBIE. Conor likes them.

(He shows the drawing he's been working on over the course of the scene to **CONOR**.*)*

See, Conor? See look, I drew more. I drew that part. See?

CONOR. Abbie.

ABBIE. Is that right? Did I get it right?

CONOR. *(reaching for it)* Dinner is soon.

ABBIE. You want it?

CONOR. Dinner is soon.

(**ABBIE** *hands* **CONOR** *the picture.*)

ABBIE. *(to* **RONNIE***)* He helped me draw that one.

RONNIE. Um, he can barely hold a *fork*, so –

ABBIE. He watched me. I was drawing an insect, like Dad said, but Conor didn't like it.

RONNIE. 'Cause it was a roach?

ABBIE. So I kept changing little things. Any time he liked something, I kept it. Any time he didn't like something, I started over. *(He gestures at the discarded drawings.)* That's what all this is.

RONNIE. So this is Conor's monster.

ABBIE. Yes – YES! That's it!

RONNIE. What is?

ABBIE. It's like…okay. Remember the Bald Woman?

RONNIE. What? No.

ABBIE. That I used to draw? You don't remember the Bald Woman?

RONNIE. I don't know. Maybe.

ABBIE. No hair, super-super-thin, her hands were like *(crooks his hands into claws)*?

RONNIE. All right, yeah. I remember.

ABBIE. You do?

RONNIE. Yeah, she was like, really sick-looking, like in a hospital gown, she was crawling…see now you're not gonna sleep tonight, why would you bring this up?

ABBIE. It scared me the most was when it looked like she was begging for something.

RONNIE. If she scared you, why did you keep drawing her?

ABBIE. *(indicating the drawing)* But this is different. The Bald Woman is *my* monster, she came from inside me.

(indicating the drawing) This is *Conor's* monster. This is what I wanna do from now on: other people's monsters. I don't wanna look at myself anymore, I hate it. So I tried looking at other people's faces, and I hated that more. But this, this is perfect. Other people's monsters. This is what's going to be my life.

RONNIE. I mean, you're fifteen. You don't have to be like "This is my life."

ABBIE. Like you're so old and wise just 'cause you got finger-blasted.

RONNIE. It makes you smarter. Seriously.

ABBIE. Thank you for kicking Jeff's ass. *(beat)*

RONNIE. Whatever.

ABBIE. Why didn't he tell them what you did?

RONNIE. He did.

ABBIE. He told them you hit him. He didn't tell them you kept kicking him while he was on the ground. If he did you'd be expelled no matter what Dad did. So why didn't he tell them?

RONNIE. I told him to. We were waiting to see the counselor, I said, "If you want me kicked out, all you have to do is tell them I put you on the ground and kicked you till you begged me to stop." All seventy pounds of me. I don't know why he didn't do it. *(pause)*

ABBIE. Hey Ronnie.

RONNIE. Good night, good night, oh my *god* goodnight.

ABBIE. I saw the Bald Woman.

RONNIE. That's great and wonderful.

ABBIE. You know where I saw her?

RONNIE. Um, nowhere, because she doesn't exist.

ABBIE. On the porch. Right outside that door.

RONNIE. I'm really happy for you.

ABBIE. She's on her knees, crawling across the porch, right outside that door. I saw her there.

RONNIE. Yeah, well, you didn't, so…

ABBIE. Then open the door. Open the door.

RONNIE. Fuck you. I'm not humoring you, okay?

ABBIE. If she's not out there on the porch, then open that door. Do it. Open it.

BILL. *(offstage)* Who is that?

RONNIE. Shit!

BILL. *(offstage)* Who's down there?

RONNIE. Get the, get the –

> *(They scurry around picking up the drawings.)*

ABBIE. Conor. Conor!

> *(But **CONOR** won't give up his picture. **BILL** appears at the top of the stairs, half-awake, in sweatpants.)*

BILL. Ronnie?

RONNIE. It's cool, Dad, it's cool, we're just hanging out.

BILL. It's…something in the morning, it's two in the morning.

RONNIE. We're drawing, we're just hanging out drawing. *(She holds up a bunch of the drawings.)*

BILL. Drawing?

RONNIE. *(handing **ABBIE** the drawings)* Here, Abbie, here's the rest of your…wonderful artworks.

BILL. It's two in the morning! Or – I think it's later than that!

RONNIE. We should be in bed!

BILL. You both have school tomorrow!

ABBIE. You go to sleep this instant, young lady.

> *(They hurry up the stairs, passing **BILL**.)*

RONNIE. You go straight to your room!

ABBIE. You go straight to *your* room!

BILL. I don't understand…

RONNIE. Goodnight Dad!

ABBIE. Goodnight Dad!

(And they're gone. **BILL** *stumbles down the stairs.)*

BILL. *(calling up the stairs behind him)* Go straight to bed!

> *(He sees* **CONOR,** *who is holding the drawing to his chest.)*

Conor? You all right? Hey, bud, what is that? Can I see that?

> *(**CONOR** starts to go for the stairs but* **BILL** *cuts him off.* **BILL** *carefully prizes the drawing from* **CONOR**'s *grip. He looks at it. He looks at* **CONOR.***)*

Who are you?

Four

*(Saturday night. **ABBIE** is drawing **RAF**. Party sounds from the next room.)*

RAF. Can I drink? Will it mess it up if I move?

ABBIE. It's fine.

RAF. Thanks for making an exception, buddy.

ABBIE. This'll be my last one.

RAF. It'll be like a collector's item.

ABBIE. If you hate the way they make you look, why do you keep asking me?

RAF. Who said that?

ABBIE. You did. Last time I drew you. You said to my dad, "Does the kid think I'm clinically depressed?"

RAF. You heard that?

*(**ABBIE** keeps drawing.)*

Maybe I like that I hate it. Are you old enough to understand that?

*(**AMELIA**, **VALERIE**, and **BELINDA** enter.)*

VALERIE. It was really delicious, Amelia.

AMELIA. Thank you, Valerie.

BELINDA. It really was, seriously.

AMELIA. Thank you, I appreciate you saying that, I was scared shitless, which…wow, I could have said that differently.

BELINDA. *(calling off)* Your wife's cursing at me Bill!

BILL. *(from the next room)* Welcome to my world!

AMELIA. What?!

BELINDA. *(to AMELIA)* Seriously, you think we were on a tin can in space for three years saying "Pass the tea"?

*(**BILL** and **KIP** enter.)*

BILL. And that's – literally, I'm talking about – that's just the first year's yield. Back me up, Val: I'm talking about the crop yield we expect from *only* the first year. The food we're going to generate in *one year* of this project.

VALERIE. Which anybody will tell you is the warm-up year. The year you expect –

KIP. Exactly, the year you're just figuring things out. It's the same in any startup.

BILL. But we're actually going to *gain*. That's my thing. That's my answer when people say, "Weren't you supposed to colonize Mars?" I say, "We were, but we got a better gig. We're going to re-imagine *Earth*."

KIP. Incredible.

VALERIE. Now Mr. Jackson, if you want to see exactly how your funds are being used –

KIP. *(to* **VALERIE***)* You can call me Kip.

VALERIE. I'm sorry?

KIP. It's just, you just called me Mr. Jackson, I just wanted to say that you could call me Kip.

VALERIE. Thank you, I will – Kip.

AMELIA. Abbie, are you sure Mr. Navares wants you drawing him?

RAF. He's sure.

BILL. *(to* **KIP***)* Now, you wanna talk about the *second* year –

AMELIA. *(to* **RAF***)* Do you want anything to eat?

RAF. Hey Bill.

AMELIA. Just, you didn't eat anything, so…

BELINDA. Seriously, Amelia, don't worry about it.

RAF. Hey Bill. Is Conor coming down? *(beat)*

KIP. Conor Wells. *That* is one man, I won't lie, that is one hand I'd like to shake.

BILL. I hear that, Kip.

KIP. I mean I understand that he's delicate, and of course I respect that – and not to forget Tom Wiley's…memory, of course.

  (Everyone's gotten quiet.)

BILL. Of course, Kip. And I know we all appreciate your saying so.

RAF. *(to* ABBIE*)* Sorry, sorry, I moved too much, right?

ABBIE. It's okay, I'm done.

RAF. Lemme see.

(He takes the drawing from ABBIE *and studies it.)*

KIP. *(to* BILL*)* That's not a bad thing is it, bringing up – if it's understood that you don't bring up Tom Wiley – or Conor –

BILL. Not at all, Kip, it's not like that.

KIP. I just know there's a lot of history, you know, among you guys, and I'm not –

VALERIE. Of course there is, but you know what? Everyone here has a role in making sure we have a beautiful world to give to our children. But we don't all have to get our hands swampy. Investors are our patron saints, Mr. Jackson. There is no Chinampas without you.

KIP. Well, like I said, "Kip." I like "get your hands swampy."

VALERIE. Of course, Kip, my apologies.

KIP. It's a good turn of phrase.

BELINDA. Yeah, you know, I thought your first name was Christopher, I've just been calling you Chris all night. You're not Chris?

KIP. It is Christopher on the birth certificate, of course, I'm just trying to make this Kip transition happen. It's all part of a sense that I'm moving into a new phase of my life –

BELINDA. Hey, I'm on board. Kip it is.

KIP. It's crazy, you know how many boards I've resigned from, just in the past year? My life was just meeting, meeting, phone call, you know, meeting…

BELINDA. Jesus *God.*

KIP. And then I saw this guy speak, right?

BILL. You're really too kind to me, Kip.

KIP. Everybody says it to you. You hear it forty times a day: when people hear you speak –

BILL. You know what, at most I'm a catalyst –

KIP. It's not just me. I'm not making this about me. If you go on the message boards –

BILL. At most I'm a catalyst. I happen to be in the right place at the right time –

KIP. It's more than that – for me it was like –

RAF. You never let me down, kid.

(He shows the drawing to **BILL**.*)*

Right? Right?

KIP. Huh. Look at that.

ABBIE. Last one, Mr. Nevares.

RAF. Too bad. You draw like a motherfucker.

ABBIE. I'm not quitting drawing, just not people. I'm drawing a comic book.

KIP. How about that? You know, I was a comic collector for a little while there.

BILL. So at any rate, with the farming sites –

KIP. What's your comic about, Abbie?

ABBIE. It's called "The Honeycomb." It's about a race of insectoid aliens that share a hive mind.

(reactions around the room)

KIP. Well. Well. Imagination, right? Runs in the family! In the genes!

AMELIA. I was thinking of opening a bottle. Would there be some demand along those lines? Red?

BILL. Yeah, um… Actually, get the one, the uh…

AMELIA. I know the one. You know, I did at one point this evening have a lovely assistant…

BILL. You did, what happened to your lovely assistant?

AMELIA. *(calling off into the kitchen)* Lovely assistant? A little assistance?

*(***RONNIE*** enters.)*

RONNIE. We're not done? We're totally done. Everyone's in here.

AMELIA. They're our guests in this room too. Maybe you'd like to take drink orders for people who don't want wine.

RONNIE. Yep, that's what I'd like to do.

(AMELIA *exits.*)

BELINDA. Wine's good.

VALERIE. I'll be fine with wine.

KIP. Yeah, I wanna hear more about this mysterious bottle!

RAF. I don't want wine.

RONNIE. Okay.

(*She looks at his drink. It's mostly full.*)

So you're good?

(RAF *downs his drink and holds out his glass.*)

RAF. No.

RONNIE. You wanna tell me what that was?

RAF. I trust you.

(RONNIE *takes the glass and exits to the kitchen.*)

BILL. (*to* RAF) Really?

RAF. "The Honeycomb"?

VALERIE. Mr. Jackson – Kip – I think you know we all feel great gratitude –

RAF. Hey so Bill, where's Conor?

VALERIE. I think you know we feel –

RAF. Is he talking yet?

BELINDA. Raf. Smoke with me. I'm going outside. Smoke with me.

RAF. (*to* BILL) What words can he use?

KIP. Is – is everything good, or –?

BILL. Yeah, I'm sorry, we're all a little –

RAF. How many words can he use?

BELINDA. Seriously, why don't you step outside with me?

VALERIE. We're all tired, why don't we –

KIP. *(to* RAF*)* Look, I hear you, man, if a friend of mine had an injury like that –

RAF. *(to* BILL*)* Bill: How many words can he use?

BILL. About twenty, Raf, which by my count is fourteen more than you. *(pause)* Kip.

KIP. Yeah, Bill, what's up?

BILL. You went to law school, right?

KIP. Yeah, yeah, of course, uh, U-Penn –

BILL. You had study groups, presumably, people, friends, you'd be studying all night.

> (RONNIE *enters with* RAF*'s drink. She watches*
> BILL *over the following.)*

KIP. Sure, definitely – actually I remember one time –

BILL. And you were in corporate law, what, eighteen years?

KIP. Almost exactly eighteen – I can't believe you remembered that –

BILL. And that too, a lot of late nights, a lot of deadlines –

KIP. Oh my god, you can't even imagine – well of course you can imagine, you were in *space*, you were all in *space* –

BILL. You know what? I bet it's not that different. Those long hours, those long nights with your co-workers, with your fellow students, trying to make something really important happen with almost no time. So of course you fight, and you make up, and you fight again, and you make up again, and you strive together, and you come out the other side, and you say, "Those assholes are the most important people in my life." You know that feeling?

KIP. I do, I guess I do.

BILL. Kip, I want you to stay. I want you to stay here all night and drink wine with us and tell stories with us and plan for this future with us. But – *(He looks at* RAF*.)* – it looks like my little band of assholes has some personal business to take care of first, so as much as it pains me personally, I think we're gonna have to have that night of wine and stories the next time. I hope you can tell from looking at my face how much I'm looking forward to it. *(pause)*

KIP. God, Bill, I don't know what to say.

BILL. Don't worry about it.

KIP. It means so much that you would say that to me.

BILL. It's just the truth.

VALERIE. Kip, the chance to get to know you tonight has been an honor.

KIP. Wow, God, I…that's amazing. I mean, I know I wasn't part of your crew, it's not like –

BILL. You're part of our new crew.

> *(As **KIP** goes around the room shaking hands, **RONNIE** brings the drink to **RAF**.)*

RONNIE. *(to **RAF**)* I hope you like it.

RAF. I love it. I want another one just like it.

RONNIE. You haven't even tried it yet.

> *(**RAF** downs the entire drink.)*

RAF. I love it. I want another one just like it.

RONNIE. Okay.

BILL. You know what, sweetheart, it's gonna be self-service from here on out. You too, Abbie.

RONNIE. All right, space people. Smoke 'em if you got 'em.

ABBIE. Good night, everybody.

RAF. *(to **RONNIE**)* You can find me online.

RONNIE. I bet.

> *(**RONNIE** and **ABBIE** leave.)*

BILL. All right, Raf –

RAF. Where the fuck is Conor?

> *(**AMELIA** enters with wine and too many glasses.)*

AMELIA. I think I may need saving here.

> *(**VALERIE** and **BILL** go to take glasses from her.)*

VALERIE. Oh, Amelia, you should have taken me with you.

AMELIA. Overestimated my capacities, I think.

BILL. Never.

AMELIA. *(about to pour)* Kip? Wanna say when?

KIP. Mrs. Cooke, I want to thank you for your hospitality tonight.

AMELIA. Oh, you're leaving?

KIP. I believe the time has come, yes. But I hope you know I'll be seeing you very soon.

AMELIA. Well I hope so.

KIP. And I hope you know – I hope you *all* know – that this has been one of the finest nights of my life.

BILL. Well, I hope you know we feel the same.

AMELIA. Let me walk you out.

KIP. Goodnight everybody.

> *(The others say goodnight, except for* **RAF**. **AMELIA** *and* **KIP** *exit through the front door.)*

BELINDA. *Jesus.*

VALERIE. Wait.

BELINDA. I thought I was just gonna have to hang myself.

VALERIE. Wait for him to leave.

BELINDA. I was like, I'm just gonna have to literally end my life, because this…

VALERIE. Wait until he drives away.

BILL. *(to RAF)* What the fuck is wrong with you?

BELINDA. Bill –

BILL. Hey! What the fuck is wrong with you?

BELINDA. He's not really hitting on Ronnie, he's just being an idiot.

BILL. Ronnie can take care of herself. I'm talking about Raf pulling out his dick and pissing on forty million dollars 'cause he's too drunk to find the bathroom.

VALERIE. He's driving away.

BILL. Do you have any idea how much we need him?

VALERIE. Amelia's coming back.

BILL. How many people are there in the world who are that rich but stupid enough to think you can save the world with experimental swamp-farming? 'Cause if we lose him you'd better find us another one!

VALERIE. Bill she's at the door.

RAF. I'd like to say hi to Conor, please.

        (**AMELIA** *enters.*)

AMELIA. He's off.

BILL. Is he all right?

AMELIA. Bill, if you break that poor girl's heart…

BILL. Yeah.

RAF. I'd like to say hi to Conor, please!

        (**BILL** *looks at* **AMELIA**.)

AMELIA. No. *(beat)* No.

BILL. You don't think…

AMELIA. Look at everybody, look around this room. Tell me he's ready for this. *(beat)* If he melts down, not only does it ruin your night…

BILL. …it's also pretty terrible for him.

RAF. I'd like to say hi to C –

BILL. Well you're not going to.

AMELIA. Be his friend, Raf.

        (*Beat.* **RAF** *moves away from them.*)

VALERIE. You've made an amazing evening for us, Amelia, and we can't begin to express our gratitude.

AMELIA. Ah. My cue.

VALERIE. Oh, I don't mean it like –

AMELIA. No, you're quite right. The space-stories hour approaches.

BELINDA. One time I was replacing this lug nut in Airlock C, it was awesome.

        (**BILL** *walks* **AMELIA** *to the stairs.*)

BILL. Milly…you know I never know the words.

AMELIA. Try to get a couple hours sleep. Seriously.

BILL. Yeah.

> (**AMELIA** *exits up the stairs.*)

VALERIE. I don't know if anyone wants refills on…?

> (*She trails off as* **BILL** *signals her to wait, listening to* **AMELIA**'s *footsteps departing.*)

BILL. The packages?

RAF. "The Honeycomb," huh?

BELINDA. In my trunk – but Bill –

RAF. A "hive mind"?

VALERIE. It's not right, Bill.

BELINDA. You told us not to prepare our people. Not that I *have* any people.

BILL. It's not preparation, it's just…

RAF. It seems like preparation.

BILL. It's just putting the idea in his mind! Guys…he's not like Ronnie. He won't just survive.

VALERIE. It's a risk. Anything's a risk.

BILL. How about this: if you get the packages I'll grovel for the rest of the night.

BELINDA. Deal.

> (*She exits out front.*)

VALERIE. Twenty words?

BILL. He's doing good.

VALERIE. Yeah?

BILL. Honestly I wanna cry some days, he's working so hard.

RAF. Who is? Who's working so hard?

BILL. Raf, for God's sake –

VALERIE. It's a fair question.

RAF. Is it Conor?

VALERIE. If not a tactful one.

RAF. Or is it the Ambassador?

BILL. You know I don't know.

RAF. If you had to guess!

BILL. I don't guess. When he knows how to talk, he'll tell us.

(**BELINDA** *returns with packages.*)

BELINDA. Should I go ahead and –?

BILL. I think maybe Raf wants to talk to us a little bit first.

VALERIE. Belinda's right, this takes priority –

BILL. Raf?

RAF. I'm struggling, man! Who wouldn't be?

BELINDA. Are you fucking kidding me?

RAF. I'm saying I don't know! Seriously, what's stupid about that?

BELINDA. It's too late for you to not know!

BILL. But that's not true though, right Raf?

RAF. What's not true?

BILL. That you don't know. That's actually not true. You know the same things we know. We all sat in the same rooms and heard the same briefings. We all know exactly how bad it is. We all know what we can do to stop it.

RAF. And I'm saying who the fuck anointed us the ones to make the choice – not just for us – for *everybody*.

VALERIE. I don't see it as a choice. I see it as a responsibility.

BILL. No, he's right. It's a choice. Sure it is. Where Raf's wrong is he's thinking about choice the way a child does. "I don't like the choice, so I just won't make it."

RAF. Fuck yourself, Bill.

BILL. The difference with a grown-up is, they understand that *not* making the choice is actually making the choice. You're just lying down and letting the choice happen to you.

RAF. I did three years just like you, just like all of you, I'm your fucking equal. I'm not your kids, so don't talk to me like I am!

BILL. Raf, right now you are the most powerful person here. You could bring this all down right now with one phone call. Now you can curse at me some more, but that's really just you putting off exercising that power. If you're gonna make the call, make the call.

VALERIE. You know what they told us. You know about the oil, you know about the population, you know about the climate shifts, you know everything that's coming.

RAF. So we do our job. We go back to Mars.

BELINDA. You were there, Raf! You worked out the time-table right along with the rest of us. There's not enough digits left on the clock. Why do we have to have this conversation for the nine-hundredth time?

BILL. We don't. Raf's as smart and as informed as anyone here. Seems to me like the thing to do is to proceed, and Raf can stop us, or help us, or disappear. Give him his package.

BELINDA. For real?

BILL. Give him his package. That way when he makes up his mind he'll already have it.

BELINDA. He can still sell us out at any point.

BILL. Then kill him and burn his body, Belinda, the choice-making applies to everyone. In the meantime, give him his package, and while you're at it, give one to everybody.

> (**BELINDA** *starts unpacking smaller bags from the larger one.*)

VALERIE. *(to* **BELINDA***)* You labeled them like I said, right?

BELINDA. One each, honeycomb size varies based on region.

BILL. And the pheromone triggers?

BELINDA. Set for remote activation. Once we install the tower, it'll all tie back to here.

RAF. Wait, what?

BILL. One switch, from here, sets off every site simultaneously. That's the idea.

RAF. I didn't know about that.

BELINDA. That's my bad, Raf. I was supposed to update you.

RAF. Wait, how is that even possible?

BILL. Valerie cracked it. *(Over the following,* **BILL** *pours wine and hands out glasses.)*

RAF. One signal? Are you running a booster?

VALERIE. It's not one signal. It originates from here, and then it passes through a network of transmitters, amplifying each time, until it releases the pheromones at each Honeycomb site. Starts the process day-and-date all over the world.

RAF. What networks? NASA? Military?

VALERIE. Mostly smaller countries. Less regs, more in need of Kip's money.

RAF. But…why go to all the extra trouble? Why trigger from here?

BILL. Raf – actually, everybody – you gotta remember, it's gonna be fast. We all saw the sample hatching, now imagine that on the scale we're talking about. Wherever any of us is when the signal goes out, that's where we're gonna be. Long-distance travel's not gonna be an option. This way, we can make sure everybody's where they want to be before I trigger.

BELINDA. What if we wanna be here?

BILL. Then, frankly, Belinda, I'll be overjoyed.

RAF. What if I wanna be here? Will you be overjoyed then?

BILL. Raf, I love you. No matter how you feel about me. I can't picture the new world without you. Without any of you. *(Pause. He holds up his glass.)* To Tom Wiley. Never forget.

RAF, BELINDA, VALERIE. Tom Wiley. *(They toast and drink.)*

BILL. Save some, Raf, there's one more. To the new world.

RAF, BELINDA, VALERIE. The new world.

(They toast and drink.)

BILL. All right. *(to* **BELINDA***)* Let's do the packages and get back to the drinking. I wanna have at least a little fun tonight.

Five

(Afternoon. **LYNN** *is playing* **AMELIA** *a recording. We hear* **BILL**'s *voice.)*

BILL. *(on the recording)* "Let's do the packages and get back to the drinking. I wanna have at least a little fun tonight."

*(***LYNN** *turns off the device.)*

LYNN. Pretty much just space stories after that point. *(beat)*

AMELIA. You did say a man can be preoccupied by something other than an affair.

LYNN. I can't make you tell me what they're talking about.

AMELIA. I'm sure you can't. I have no idea.

*(***LYNN** *is taking something out of her bag.)*

What is that?

LYNN. A transcript. Bill says –

AMELIA. You made a transcript?

LYNN. "We all sat in the same rooms and heard the same briefings." Do you know what briefings he's talking about?

AMELIA. They were all in briefings all the time, especially leading up to launch, but I don't know specifically which briefings –

LYNN. Did he ever talk to you about what they briefed him on?

AMELIA. Not about Mars. That was classified.

LYNN. Who was briefing them?

AMELIA. Also classified, apparently.

LYNN. What classified stuff do they need to tell astronauts?

AMELIA. I just know what he said.

LYNN. "The oil," "the population," "the climate shifts."

AMELIA. I certainly know what the *words* mean.

LYNN. "Pheromone triggers." A "sample hatching."

AMELIA. You can keep throwing these terms at me –

LYNN. "Long-distance travel's not gonna be an option."

AMELIA. What do you want me to say?

LYNN. All right, look... I set up this meeting so I could tell you I'm out.

AMELIA. Out?

LYNN. I'll charge you a couple days expenses, forget the rest.

AMELIA. All right.

LYNN. I'm not a cop. I take pictures of guys sneaking into Sheratons. Loose ends don't keep me awake at night.

AMELIA. I understand.

LYNN. This is so *fucked*! Listen to them, they're not kidding, there's not the slightest indication that they're...but what's the alternative? They're all crazy? All four of them? Honored, decorated astronauts?

AMELIA. Lynn, is my husband some kind of – I feel ridiculous!

LYNN. Let's not use any words. *(beat)* I'll walk away if you want. I won't like it, but I'll walk.

AMELIA. Don't. *(pause)*

LYNN. I can't wire up Chinampas. The security there, it's beyond me.

AMELIA. So...

LYNN. Can you get them to be here, more?

AMELIA. To what, to do their work here?

LYNN. If they're talking here we can listen.

AMELIA. Why would they work here? Their equipment, everything's at Chinampas.

LYNN. What kind of equipment?

AMELIA. I don't know.

LYNN. What, that's classified too? It's a charity, right?

AMELIA. Well, it's a foundation –

LYNN. What about the Chinampas Everglades preserve, an hour from here, have you seen it?

AMELIA. No, only the crew's allowed –

LYNN. No, of course you haven't seen it. Why would they risk national security by letting you see a *farm*?

AMELIA. I don't understand, what's wrong with you?

LYNN. This is okay with you? This is fine to be your life? Married to a guy who tells you nothing? I'd lose my mind in a week! Sorry, sorry that's…not helpful. Shit.

AMELIA. No, it's like…talking to my daughter in ten years. It's good practice.

LYNN. What are you up for here?

AMELIA. What do you need?

LYNN. Off the bat, two things. Number one, we need those people in this house talking where I can hear. Any way you can think to get them here, you pounce on it. Number two, we need to find out how scared we need to be.

AMELIA. How do we do that?

LYNN. You need to get him talking about the future. Your marriage, your kids, anything. Anything to remind him what he has and what he can lose. I wanna know if he can contemplate the future. I wanna know if he can talk about it at all.

Six

(Late at night. **ABBIE** *is drawing.* **CONOR** *is in his corner, watching him.* **ABBIE** *stops drawing and looks at* **CONOR**.*)*

ABBIE. What's up? Are you okay?*(He slowly rises.)* Can I come over to you? Do you want to come over to me?

*(***CONOR** *holds his arms out.)*

What?

*(***CONOR** *gestures more emphatically with his arms.)*

Wait…

CONOR. Hhhlp.

ABBIE. You wanna practice?

CONOR. Hehlp.

ABBIE. Are you sure? You're walking pretty well now.

*(***CONOR** *gestures again.)*

All right. I don't mind.

*(***ABBIE** *steps into a straight line with* **CONOR** *and holds his arms out.* **CONOR** *walks a little unsteadily until he reaches* **ABBIE** *and then grabs hold of his arms.)*

Okay…hold on to the chair…you got it?

*(***CONOR** *holds on to the chair.)*

CONOR. *(gesturing to go again)* Hhhelp.

ABBIE. Okay, fine, let's do another one.

(He crosses the room and holds his arms out. **CONOR** *walks to him – mostly steadily – and grabs his arms.)*

See, I actually think you're faking. You can totally walk.

*(***CONOR** *gestures for* **ABBIE** *to cross the room. With good humor.)*

No, you're being ridiculous. You're just being goofy.

CONOR. *(gesturing to go again)* Hhhelp.

ABBIE. *(crossing the room)* Fine, Goofy McGooferson.

> *(He holds his arms out. CONOR crosses toward him.)*

You know what? I'm gonna be like Mom. I'm gonna...

> *(As CONOR almost reaches him he backs away.)*

Like that. And a little more...

> *(CONOR almost gets to ABBIE, but ABBIE steps back again.)*

Like that. Keep coming, you can do it...

> *(He backs away again. CONOR stumbles just slightly, but reaches ABBIE again.)*

Perfect. Perfect.

> *(They look at each other.)*

What? What? It's okay. What?

CONOR. Abbie.

> *(They stay still for a beat, holding each other's arms.)*

ABBIE. When people touch me? I hate it. You're lucky. When people touch you, you can just scream and it's okay.

> *(CONOR backs away.)*

No, it's fine, it's fine. Don't be sorry.

CONOR. Abbie.

ABBIE. Don't be sorry. I'm the same.

> *(The front door opens. RONNIE enters. She speaks to someone outside that we can't see. ABBIE and CONOR quickly separate. Over the following CONOR returns to his corner.)*

RONNIE. Wait outside a second.

> *(a male voice, not quite intelligible)*

RONNIE. No, seriously, wait outside. *(She closes the door and sees* **ABBIE.***)* See this is what I'm saying.

ABBIE. What?

> *(***RONNIE*** runs a bit up the stairs to listen.* **ABBIE** *looks at the front door.)*

Is there somebody there?

RONNIE. Abbie. I got it. *(She goes to the door.)* Okay, it looks like they're asleep, so…but you've gotta be *quiet. (to* **ABBIE***)* Some night I want to come home to this living room and not find you here.

ABBIE. It's not my job to make it easier for you to sneak around.

> *(***RAF*** enters. He's inebriated, but controlling it.)*

Oh – Mr. Nevares? I think – wait…were you looking for… I think my Dad's…

> *(***RAF***, amused, indicates that he can't talk.)*

RONNIE. Jesus Christ, Abbie.

ABBIE. I'm sorry. I'm sorry. I was going to bed. I was just finishing up. We were – I was – I was drawing some things, but… I finished.

> *(***RAF*** nods with exaggerated sadness, and waves.)*

So, so, um, Ronnie, I'll see you…tomorrow?

RONNIE. Probably, yeah.

ABBIE. Conor, do you wanna go up?

RAF. *(realizing* **CONOR** *is there)* Shit!

ABBIE. Do you wanna go up or stay down? Either one's cool.

CONOR. Abbie.

RAF. Oh Jesus.

ABBIE. Stay down?

RONNIE. Abbie, come on, take him up.

ABBIE. He doesn't want to. I can't make him. You want him to flip out?

RONNIE. Conor, Abbie's going up. Don't you wanna go with Abbie? Go up?

CONOR. Ronnie home.

RONNIE. Whoa. That's new.

ABBIE. No it's not. That's one of his words now.

RONNIE. Since when?

ABBIE. Since, like, a week.

RONNIE. So, if you're not a member of the Obsessed With Conor Club, it's new.

ABBIE. Fuck you, Ronnie. Goodnight, Mr. Nevares. *(ABBIE exits up the stairs.)*

RONNIE. God!

RAF. *(fixed on CONOR)* Oh man, buddy, fuck.

RONNIE. I can't even, like, raise my voice him. I talk to my friends like that all the time!

RAF. *(to CONOR)* Fuck, man, I don't know what to…

RONNIE. Why are we here? This is stupid. Where do you live?

RAF. It doesn't scare you?

RONNIE. What?

RAF. Him just standing in the dark like that?

RONNIE. That's where he always is. Unless he's in bed.

RAF. So you're just…used to it?

RONNIE. I mean, it's been years.

RAF. *(walking closer to CONOR)* Hey man, I… I didn't think I was gonna… *(to RONNIE)* Does he know what I'm saying?

RONNIE. Not all the *words*, but like – maybe tone down the *vibe* –

RAF. You know what's hilarious, right?

RONNIE. Okay, you have to be quiet.

RAF. What's hilarious is, I did two major missions with this guy before either one of us ever met your Dad. Three missions together in tin cans in space before we ever heard the name Bill Cooke. You know what space is?

RONNIE. You mean like the science?

RAF. Space is the tightest embrace there is. Because it's death. It's colder than anything, it's actually *nothing*, and it's *death*, you can see it through the window, wrapped tight all around you, no compromise. So when you're in the steel box with somebody, and space is outside, that means you live inside death together. That's more than a friend, that's everything. We'd get back and it'd be like, "Fuck off, dude, I need a big long break from your face," but honestly, one week would go by, and one of us would call, and the other one would just pick up and say, "Tell me where."

RONNIE. Wait, so why haven't you –

RAF. *(to CONOR)* And then you got…hurt, or whatever that was…you know you don't always have to step up, right? Every single time? "I got it, sir." Keep saying "I got it, sir," eventually, you're gonna say that about the wrong fucking job. I *told* you.

RONNIE. All right, um, Raf?

RAF. And I knew where they had you, and I knew I could go, your folks signed a paper, but it was like… "Well, let me just take care of this, take care of that," and then I'd look up and visiting hours were over. I did that every day for *months*. Until I finally *go* and they're like "No, he lives with Bill Cooke now. You knew him first, but he lives with Bill Cooke now."

RONNIE. You know what?

RAF. *(to CONOR)* What do you want me to say? "I'm sorry"? I don't know *what* I am!

RONNIE. …and I think we're done.

RAF. *(to CONOR)* I don't know what *you* are. *(realizes what* RONNIE *said)* Wait. What? Wait. Come on. I'm over it, I'm over it, that was just a blip, that was just an interval, I'm back.

RONNIE. I mean…

RAF. I'm good! Look at my face, I'm good, I'm all the way back! C'mere.

RONNIE. Seriously?

> (**RAF** *pulls* **RONNIE** *close and starts kissing her.*
> *She's dubious, but starts responding. Then* **RAF**
> *sees* **CONOR** *again.*)

RAF. Look, can we put him in another room, or –

RONNIE. All right. Good night.

RAF. We put him in another room! We walk him like four
feet, through there –

RONNIE. You can't touch him.

RAF. It's like ten steps to the kitchen – I'll do it.

RONNIE. I mean it, you can't touch him.

RAF. I can't walk him a couple feet through that door?

> (**RONNIE** *gets between* **RAF** *and* **CONOR**.)

Seriously? You're protecting my best friend from me?

RONNIE. You can't just touch him, he's sick, okay?

RAF. You don't know what he is.

RONNIE. Out. Now.

RAF. You don't know what he is, you don't even know –
Conor. *(He tries to shove past her.)* Conor. Or whoever you
are. Who are you? Conor!

> (*He tries to shove past* **RONNIE** *again. She punches*
> *him in the solar plexus.* **RAF** *goes down.*)

RONNIE. Get your breath and get out.

> (*She quickly goes to* **CONOR** *before he can freak*
> *out.*)

Conor? Are you good? Do you wanna go up?

CONOR. Abbie.

RONNIE. Abbie's up. Do you wanna go up?

CONOR. Up.

RAF. Fuck…the fuck am I doing?

RONNIE. You're driving home drunk. Drive slowly.

Seven

(Morning. AMELIA enters from the kitchen.)

AMELIA. *(calling upstairs)* I'm sorry, is anyone eating this morning? At all? If no one's eating I can go back to bed, right? *(BILL comes running down the stairs.)*

BILL. *(on a cell phone)* Right, but you see the problem? I have to actually *be* there right now, if I'm gonna accomplish anything today... I've fed him every excuse I have! – all right, I'm sorry, go ahead.

> *(AMELIA tries to get BILL's attention. He indicates that he can't talk.)*

Wait, what? Okay. Start again from the beginning.

AMELIA. Are you hungry?

> *(BILL indicates again that he can't talk. RONNIE comes down the stairs.)*

Hey – *hey.* There's waffles.

RONNIE. Gotta go.

AMELIA. You don't want any breakfast before you go to school?

RONNIE. *Jesus!*

> *(RONNIE goes past AMELIA and shoves through the door into the kitchen.)*

BILL. *(on the phone)* Well, who is she? Who's she with?

AMELIA. *(calling up the stairs)* Abbie! *(She realizes the futility and starts up the stairs.)*

BILL. Well shit, I mean, should I come in at all?

> *(AMELIA hears this and stops.)*

I'm asking for your judgment. I trust your judgment.

> *(AMELIA comes back downstairs.)*

Okay, well, it's two issues, right? One is, is it happening, and how do we find out? Two is – they can? That's a thing, they can *scan* for it? Remotely? And you trust them?

(AMELIA signals BILL. He waves her away.)

How soon could they do it?

(She mouths: "Work from home." BILL turns away from her.)

How do you have this many people owing you favors?

(AMELIA gets his attention again.)

Hang on Val.

(to AMELIA)

Okay seriously?

AMELIA. Work from home.

BILL. I don't get it.

AMELIA. Get Val, get whoever, get them to come out here.

BILL. You're kidding.

AMELIA. If there's a problem at the office – I'm not listening to your call, I was just in the room –

BILL. It's just a thing, it's too boring to explain –*(to the phone)* Yeah yeah, one sec, Val.

AMELIA. So work from home. Bring whoever. I'll make something or order something.

BILL. You'll make something?

AMELIA. Or order something, depending on my energy level. Or largesse. It'll be a treat.

BILL. I sense a trap.

AMELIA. Why would you say that?

BILL. Nothing, I'm trying to be humorous or something – are you serious?

AMELIA. And maybe, I was thinking…

BILL. What.

AMELIA. I was just thinking we're kind of overdue for a date night. *(beat)*

BILL. Well, I mean, probably yeah.

AMELIA. I was thinking that.

BILL. Well, we should – are you serious?

AMELIA. Why do you keep asking that?

BILL. I'm not, I withdraw it. Um…we'll figure it out tonight, we'll schedule it tonight.

AMELIA. All right.

BILL. All right! This is good.

AMELIA. Tell Val hi.

BILL. *(remembering the phone)* Val – yeah. Yeah. No – change of plans. We're gonna do a field day.

> *(He exits to the kitchen, passing **RONNIE**, who is entering with a waffle in a Ziploc bag.)*

AMELIA. All right – I'm sorry – a waffle in a bag?

RONNIE. My ride's coming.

AMELIA. You can sit down for three minutes and eat a waffle off a plate, right?

RONNIE. Ming-Chu's picking me up in like forty seconds. Bye.

AMELIA. Ask her in, I like Ming-Chu.

RONNIE. Awesome, maybe you can beg her for a date night too. *(pause)*

AMELIA. You know what? It can go the other way too. I can suddenly decide one day I don't respect you either. It's not a biological imperative, I can not respect you right back.

> *(**RONNIE** storms out the front door. After a beat, **AMELIA** goes up the stairs.)*

Abbie!

Eight

(Day. **BILL**, **VALERIE**, *and* **BELINDA** *have laptops and papers spread out.* **CONOR** *is in his corner.)*

BILL. And I'm sorry, that's the Okavango site we're talking about.

BELINDA. Yeah, Okavango. I could show you on the live feed if we were at Chinampas.

BILL. Just tell me if we're happy.

BELINDA. We're totally happy: conditions in the preserve are holding, the honeycomb's intact and responding, the primary and backup receivers are ready for distribution and terraforming.

BILL. So what does that leave?

BELINDA. Iraqi Marshlands, Tigris-Euphrates.

BILL. Raf.

VALERIE. Yeah.

BILL. And if I ask if he's called in, you'll say, "If he had, why wouldn't I tell you?"

VALERIE. I like to think I wouldn't be snippy about it.

BILL. What about his signal beacon?

VALERIE. We can't check that from here.

BELINDA. Which begs the question, why are we here?

*(***BILL** *and* **VALERIE** *look at each other.)*

VALERIE. Jackson's waiting at Chinampas reception.

BELINDA. What – Kip?

VALERIE. Someone hassling him, some woman.

BELINDA. What woman?

VALERIE. Let me do my thing.

BILL. Look, we just need Raf to confirm, right? Every other site is set.

VALERIE. That's right.

BELINDA. What if we go without knowing about Tigris-Euphrates?

VALERIE. It's conceivable, but we risk losing the hive a key beachhead in the Middle East – and remember, that's gonna be one of the biggest terraform jobs post-transition.

BILL. I won't trigger until Raf's squared away.

VALERIE. I know how you feel.

BILL. He'd be totally alone. He wouldn't know anyone.

BELINDA. It's gonna be that way for a lot of people.

BILL. We don't go without Raf. We're not talking about this.

(**VALERIE**'s phone rings.)

VALERIE. My contact.

(**BILL** nods; **VALERIE** exits to the kitchen.)

BELINDA. So we're what, hiding out? Laying low?

BILL. It's fun, it's like camp. Plus Milly's cooking.

BELINDA. That quiche thing again?

BILL. Maybe, maybe not. She sort of wanders the farmer's market, looking for inspiration.

BELINDA. You know what I've been doing?

BILL. I can't even guess.

BELINDA. I'm trying to get ready, you know, trying to get my mind conditioned? It's like the brain I'm gonna need to pull this off is not the brain I'm gonna need when it's done.

BILL. Yeah, I think that a lot.

BELINDA. Right now we have to think about a million things at once, but after…

BILL. How do we go from sixty to, like, *two*, yeah.

BELINDA. So I garden, a few hours a night. For practice.

BILL. Wait, are you serious?

BELINDA. What, motherfucker? I garden. No music, no cell phone, just garden.

BILL. That's actually brilliant.

(**VALERIE** re-enters.)

BILL. Hey Val, are you aware we're in the presence of a green-thumbed wonder –

> *(He breaks off as he sees that* **VALERIE** *is typing furiously on her tablet.)*

BELINDA. What?

> *(***BILL*** *indicates for* **BELINDA** *to be quiet.* **VALERIE** *hands* **BILL** *the tablet. He reads, passes it to* **BELINDA**. **VALERIE** *indicates that* **BILL** *needs to talk.)*

BILL. Yeah, apparently Belinda here has taken up gardening. *(takes tablet back, types)* It's quite a...quite a...

VALERIE. As in...vegetables?

BELINDA. Nah, dude, weed. Yeah, vegetables!

BILL. *(handing the tablet to* **VALERIE**) Have any vegetables actually appeared?

> *(***VALERIE*** *and* **BELINDA** *read.)*

Like if I come over I'll see actual crops?

> *(The three of them begin searching the living room for a listening device.)*

BELINDA. *(as* **VALERIE** *writes)* Um, what do you call tomatoes, carrots...um...beets...corn...

BILL. Corn? You're telling me there's six foot...stalks...in your backyard...

VALERIE. I don't think I saw you eat a vegetable the whole time I've known –

> *(***BILL*** *signals for her to be quiet. He's thinking. A beat.)*

BILL. Why don't you just come in? Whoever you are. Obviously we're gonna get rid of your device now we know it's here, so you won't be able to listen anymore, so why don't you just come in and say hello? We're retired astronauts. We're not the Mafia. Why don't we just talk?

> *(to* **VALERIE** *and* **BELINDA**)

Let's give it a minute.

BELINDA. Is there like…a plan?

BILL. Close it up. Close everything up.

> (*They hurry around closing laptops.* **LYNN** *enters with her hand in her pocket.*)

LYNN. I'm armed.

VALERIE. That's lovely.

BILL. Do you want to sit down?

LYNN. Everybody stay where I can see you!

> (*She senses someone behind her, whirls around with her gun halfway out when she sees that it's* **CONOR.**)

Jesus.

BELINDA. Shit, she is armed.

BILL. I'd love it if you wouldn't shoot my stroke-victim friend. Or anybody.

LYNN. Stay where I can see you!

BILL. Wouldn't this be easier with backup?

LYNN. It's coming.

VALERIE. She does match Kip's description.

LYNN. Okay, my wire's not in pieces on the floor, so how do you even know it's here?

BILL. That's interesting, so when you shook down our poor benefactor Kip Jackson –

LYNN. You'd have to have a scanner. Or know someone with a scanner.

BILL. When you led him to believe that you were affiliated with some sort of government agency, you didn't have any backup then either.

LYNN. Backup's coming!

BILL. Well, do you wanna ask questions now, or wait for your backup to get here?

LYNN. You know what I wanna know.

BILL. No, I don't, truly. To know that I'd have to know who you are, who you're with, and how you even had the idea of tapping my living room in the first place.

LYNN. "We all sat in the same rooms and heard the same briefings."

BILL. I'm sorry?

LYNN. "You know about the oil, you know about the population, you know the climate shifts, you know everything that's coming."

BILL. What am I missing?

VALERIE. They're quotes. Things we said in this room.

LYNN. What briefings are you talking about?

(BILL *and* VALERIE *look at each other.*)

VALERIE. *(to* BILL*)* Jesus.

BILL. I mean, considering what we're already signed up for…

LYNN. 'Cause nobody needs a super-secret briefing to know the oil's running out, or the population's exploding.

BILL. You do if you want to know how fast it's happening.

LYNN. So this is what, eco-terrorism? That's the thing?

BELINDA. "Eco-terrorism"?

LYNN. Want me to do one for you? "Conditions in the preserve are holding, the honeycomb's intact and responding, the primary and backup receivers are ready for distribution and terraforming."

VALERIE. Photographic memory?

LYNN. I wasn't born with it; I had to practice. Now "Terraform" means take another planet and make it more like Earth, right?

BELINDA. Sure, that's like, the children's version.

LYNN. But all thirteen Chinampas swamp preserves, far-flung as they are, they're all, y'know, *on Earth.*

BILL. *(to* VALERIE*)* I mean, tell me if I'm wrong.

LYNN. How can you Terraform something that's already on Earth?

VALERIE. *(to* **BILL***)* You're not wrong.

LYNN. Don't look at her, look at me.

BILL. You can't. The term is a placeholder. They don't have a name for their planet, so there's no prefix to swap in for "Terra."

BELINDA. Shit, Bill.

LYNN. Okay, wait a minute…

BILL. *(to* **BELINDA***)* She can quote chapter and verse. There's no sweet-talking this.

LYNN. So when you say Terraforming…

VALERIE. *(to* **BILL***)* What do you want to do?

BILL. *(approaching* **LYNN***)* I'll tell you what – what's your name again?

LYNN. Stay where you are.

BILL. Why don't you give me the gun?

LYNN. Why don't you stay where you are?

BILL. Or just put it on the table, where we can all see it. I think we'd all be happier if you –

LYNN. I don't care about making you happy.

BELINDA. Bill I seriously think this bitch might shoot.

BILL. I don't.

> *(He moves closer. She draws the gun. Behind her,* **CONOR** *gets agitated.)*

LYNN. I'm not fucking kidding!

CONOR. Bill!

> *(***RAF** *quietly enters behind* **LYNN***.)*

BILL. It's okay, bud, Dinner is soon. *(to* **LYNN***)* See the smart move would be to run, but if you run you'll never know, and you really want to know.

> *(***RAF** *moves closer to* **LYNN***.)*

LYNN. You think you got me figured out? Take one more step.

CONOR. Bill, Bill when is dinner!?

LYNN. *(turning to* CONOR, *about to see* RAF*)* Tell this guy to –
    hey!

    *(*RAF *seizes* LYNN.*)*

CONOR. When is dinner!?

    *(*BILL *steps in and wrests the gun away from*
    LYNN.*)*

LYNN. Get the fuck off me!

BILL. *(raising the gun)* Get away from her.

    *(*RAF *flings* LYNN *away from him, gets out of the
    gun's way.* BILL *keeps the gun on her.)*

(to CONOR*)* Dinner is soon, bud, dinner is soon. You see
    how I'm okay? I'm okay.

CONOR. Dinner is soon.

BILL. Dinner is soon.

LYNN. I'll scream. A lot.

BILL. You scream, I have to shoot.

LYNN. I'm betting not. HELP! HELLLLP!

BELINDA. Fucking shoot her!

    *(*BILL *holds out the gun to her.)*

LYNN. HELLLLLP!

BILL. Take it!

    *(*BELINDA *takes the gun.)*

BELINDA. What, you want me to shoot her?

LYNN. I'm BEING HELD PRISONER IN THE COOKE
    FAMILY –

    *(*BILL *punches her in the jaw, knocking her out.)*

BILL. Punch with your whole body.

    *(*VALERIE *crouches by* LYNN, *examining her.)*

CONOR. When is dinner?

RAF. *(to* CONOR, *sadly)* Dinner is soon, Conor.

    *(*CONOR *looks at him, interested. To* BILL.*)*

I saw you in the window. I didn't think you saw me.

BILL. I couldn't risk it. If she'd seen me signal you she would've bolted.

BELINDA. Where the shit have you been?

(VALERIE scrolls through LYNN's phone contacts.)

RAF. Site Seven, Iraqi Marshlands, where do you think?

BILL. Did you have any idea how worried we were?

BELINDA. Fuck worried, how's the site?

RAF. Conditions holding, receivers ready, good to go for terraforming. All good.

VALERIE. Bill. *(She hands BILL the cell phone.)* In her contacts. Under "A."

(BILL reads.)

BILL. *(handing the phone to BELINDA)* Does anybody remember exactly when Amelia left for the farmer's market?

VALERIE. Thirty-two minutes ago.

(BELINDA hands RAF the phone, which he reads.)

BILL. Where are we at, Raf?

RAF. *(partly to CONOR)* I'm all in. It's the only way I can think to make it mean something.

(BILL nods, studying RAF.)

BILL. *(to RAF)* It has to be you. Amelia doesn't know you're back, she won't think it's strange if you're not here for supper. *(He hands RAF the gun.)* Compared to what's coming?

RAF. I got it.

BILL. A drop in the bucket. Not even.

RAF. Yeah – Bill – I got it.

VALERIE. *(to BILL)* Where?

BILL. Where else? The Everglades Site. The Honeycomb.

RAF. I'll pull the car up. *(He exits out the front door.)*

VALERIE. Raf.

(She finds LYNN*'s keys and presses the button. A car beeps in acknowledgement outside.)*

Take her car.

*(*RAF *takes the keys and exits. To* BILL*)*

We have to accelerate everything.

BILL. This week. It has to be this week.

BELINDA. Well, awesome, right?

BILL. *(to* BELINDA*)* How fast can we move the transmitter into this room?

BELINDA. Like in the trunk of a car? Five trips.

BILL. Okay, two trips tonight, three tomorrow, all after dark. Is that too much?

BELINDA. Not for *me*, but what about the wife and kids?

VALERIE. Yeah, Bill, what *about* the wife and kids?

BILL. All right: everybody needs to decide *now* where they wanna be after. If it's not here, you need to start looking up flights. We're almost there. *(to* BELINDA*)* I'll get under her shoulders; you'll get her legs?

BELINDA. Yeah.

BILL. *(to* CONOR*)* You okay, buddy?

CONOR. Dinner is soon.

(lights down)

End of Act One

ACT TWO

Nine

*(Early evening. **BILL** is closing his pants and hunting around for his shirt. **AMELIA** enters in a robe. They look at each other, grinning.)*

BILL. So, uh… Hello.

AMELIA. Hello.

BILL. I'm afraid I'm at a loss.

AMELIA. That's okay. *(They kiss.)*

BILL. You think we woke up Conor?

AMELIA. You can't hear anything up there.

BILL. Where did that come from? I mean, it's been a while, but *that*…

AMELIA. I'm not questioning it.

BILL. Well I think we should. I think we should intellectualize it. By talking.

AMELIA. Oh yeah?

BILL. I'm a talker.

AMELIA. I think that's what we discovered tonight.

BILL. *(crossing to the kitchen door)* Shit, you know what? There's a hostess at a Vietnamese restaurant wondering where we are right now. I'm gonna let them know we're – wanna say twenty minutes?

AMELIA. Sure.

> *(**BILL** exits into the kitchen. After a beat, **AMELIA** finds her phone and makes a call. No answer. Glancing at the kitchen, she gets a plastic bag out of her bag and empties the contents – brochures – on the table.)*

BILL. *(offstage)* I think we're good!

AMELIA. Okay!

> *(She spreads the brochures around and then moves away just as* **BILL** *re-enters.)*

BILL. Yeah, they said it's fine.

AMELIA. Good.

BILL. So do you want to…get dressed?

AMELIA. Yeah. *(She's not moving.)*

BILL. Okay.

AMELIA. It was good, wasn't it?

BILL. Are you… I mean, yeah, it was, of course it was.

AMELIA. We still have that. That's still there. I guess it's never stopped being there.

BILL. Hey, that's why I picked you. Over all my other suitors.

AMELIA. Picked me?

BILL. I'm sorry, wrong words, I'm just, bantering or something.

AMELIA. Is that how you remember it happening? That there was a moment where you picked me?

BILL. Milly…

AMELIA. I'm sorry.

BILL. Well you don't have to be sorry, it's just…you know what, we don't have to go there.

AMELIA. No, I'll get dressed.

BILL. No, come on, that's ridiculous, it's our night, why should we sit around doing things we don't want to do?

AMELIA. No, I mean, we made reservations –

BILL. Who cares? Let's go somewhere stupid. What was that place with those horrible glowy drinks? Let's go somewhere ridiculous and talk about anything we want.

AMELIA. We can talk about anything we want here, too.

BILL. All right, yes.

AMELIA. The kids are gone.

BILL. You're right. I just thought, we're always here, so… although I guess you might now respond that *I'm* not always here.

AMELIA. No, no, I'm not trying to –

BILL. I'm sorry, can I just say something?

AMELIA. *God*, I feel like I'm ruining this and –

BILL. I haven't touched anyone but you the whole time we've been married. Actually forget married, I haven't touched anyone but you since we got serious, what was it, six dates in? That's not something you should have to wonder about, but, yeah, it's been a really long time. And I come home late. So I thought maybe I should say something like there's no one but you. *(beat)* Are you – what's happening?

AMELIA. I don't know, I don't know, I feel like…

BILL. Jesus, Milly.

AMELIA. Like, fight or flight or something.

BILL. Do you want me to touch you or not touch you?

AMELIA. Don't say anything for a minute. *(pause)* I thought: The next time we have sex it'll be bad sex. 'Cause we're so far apart from each other. And then it wasn't. *(pause)*

BILL. I come home late. I keep secrets from you.

AMELIA. Yeah.

BILL. I went into space for three years, and then I came back and said, "I'm not an astronaut anymore."

AMELIA. And I know your work is important, what you all do, I'm not saying it isn't –

BILL. But it's kinda weird I'd spend all those years getting as far as I did and then just stop.

AMELIA. I don't know how to ask you things. I lost the habit.

BILL. The briefings, right?

AMELIA. For almost two years before Mars. You couldn't say, so I couldn't ask, so I…got used to not asking. You'd come home, lock your papers in the safe, and the first thing you'd say:

BILL. "Well, that's enough about me, how did Ronnie get in trouble today?"

AMELIA. For almost two years.

BILL. So at two briefings a week, minus vacations, that would've been close to two hundred briefings. That I told you nothing about.

AMELIA. And I understand that, I do, I just –

BILL. That many briefings over that much time, after a while it stops being about information and starts being about tone. How it changes, over time, from professional neutrality to unprofessional panic: huge climate fluctuations, record temperatures reported around the world, overestimated fuel reserves, markets on the edge of collapse, an exploding global underclass just sitting on the hot curb all day long.

AMELIA. How does any of that train you to go to Mars?

BILL. At the beginning it was, "We salute you, brave explorers of the last frontier." By the end it was, "You're our getaway. We're counting on you." One day you're a pioneer, the next day you're an advance man.

AMELIA. Getaway?

BILL. Pretend someone said to you, a couple weeks before launch, "Go to Mars, take this equipment, run your tests just like you were planning…but just for the heck of it, just for laughs, bring us back a timeline for how quickly we could, if necessary, rapidly relocate choice personnel to a secure Mars-based facility." What would that make you think?

AMELIA. I don't know.

BILL. What would you go home and say to your wife? About your day? To your kids? I'd walk in the house, you'd say "The principal called about Ronnie again," and I wanted to say: "*Good.* God love her. I hope she burned the goddam school down."

AMELIA. So for the whole three years on the *Celeste*…

BILL. Yeah, how's that for a conversation starter? "Rapidly relocate choice personnel." The six of us, sitting around, hashing out every possible explanation. Did they really think we were gonna come back the same people? *(beat)* Milly, I swear to God, I really need you to tell me if this is right. Is this right? Is this helping? 'Cause if I lost –

AMELIA. *(breaks away)* Look at me, I'm still in a robe, let me –

BILL. It's fine, what are you –

AMELIA. No, I'll get dressed, can we still make it?

BILL. I mean, we don't have to go right this second –

AMELIA. *(heading up the stairs)* No, I'm fine, just give me two minutes –

BILL. *(His eyes fall on the brochures.)* What's this?

AMELIA. I meant to clean those up.

BILL. Wait these – these are all for Ronnie?

AMELIA. She doesn't even look at them, so I keep them.

BILL. These are really good schools.

AMELIA. She makes really good grades, when she's not in detention.

BILL. Amazing, right? We've got two kids, and which one do I sit up at night worrying about? The one who's never been to detention. The one whose teachers basically worship him.

AMELIA. Or resent him.

BILL. Which is just as good.

AMELIA. I always think – and it's stupid, I know we've talked about it, but I still…like did I do something, at some point, that I didn't even…?

BILL. No – Milly – Abbie is who he is.

AMELIA. He just bruises so easily.

BILL. He is who he is. What did you do with him you didn't do with Ronnie? We have a huge effect on them, sure, but at a certain point, they're born people. They're already somebody. He is who he is, he's beautiful.

AMELIA. He's so beautiful. I make myself crazy picturing all the people who won't agree.

BILL. What people?

AMELIA. *(watching* **BILL***)* That he'll deal for the rest of his life.

BILL. Yeah.

> *(Beat.* **AMELIA** *comes back down the stairs.)*

AMELIA. So what's your pick?

BILL. My pick?

AMELIA. If it was up to you. Say they all accepted her. Which one would you pick?

BILL. I don't know, Milly, I'm just seeing these now.

AMELIA. Somewhere near? Somewhere far?

BILL. Okay, near.

AMELIA. Why?

BILL. So we could see her. What do you mean? So we could see her every day.

AMELIA. You wouldn't want her to make her own life?

BILL. Well she doesn't have to forsake her family to have her own life.

AMELIA. Well, I'm not talking about "forsaking her family –"

BILL. What does that mean, her own life? There is no "her own life." There's only one life. We all live in it together.

AMELIA. What do you think this is? *(brandishes some brochures)* Whether it's one of these or none of them, this is *her own life* coming at us a million miles an hour! And then that snotty, hateful little shit is gonna leave us.

BILL. All right, Milly.

AMELIA. And in a couple more years – and I bet they'll be short ones – these'll start saying "Abbie" on them. And then it'll be just us.

BILL. And Conor.

AMELIA. And you'll have to remember why you picked me.

BILL. I'm sorry. Totally wrong words, I don't know what I was –

AMELIA. No, they're not, you did pick me. Let's tell the truth. You picked me out of any number of people and then I didn't really turn out.

BILL. What the fuck are you talking about?

AMELIA. I talked big, and then it was Ronnie, then Abbie, then Conor, and now it's years on, and I'm this person who leaves the house for groceries or when somebody misses the bus, and I'm too old to start anything now.

BILL. You didn't feel yourself gliding past it just now? Ronnie, Abbie, Conor? They're your masterpiece.

AMELIA. Oh, "masterpiece," for god's –

BILL. Yes, masterpiece, don't say it like that! Why did I pick you? I didn't pull your name out of a hat, I was in awe of you. You could do this amazing thing: you could choose a thing to do, and concentrate on doing it until it was done, and let everything else go. I could never do that. I do fifty things at once and I never slow down, but you, hunkered down on that floor with them, making them walk, making them read, hours at a stretch, unbroken. That's how life is supposed to be lived: have a worthy task, devote yourself to it, and let everything else go. *That's* what we're here to do, but instead we just dribble ourselves everywhere. Only once in my life did I have what you have: those three years in space. 'Cause there was no choice. Wake up, do the work, relax with my loved ones, go to sleep. You do it without thinking about it. But I could only do it when I didn't have a choice. How did I go three years up there without you? I didn't. In my *life*, I never felt more like you were there. *(They embrace.)*

AMELIA. So we've screwed this up pretty good.

BILL. I mean, I don't know…

AMELIA. I'm gonna be honest, this isn't the hottest, sexiest conversation I've ever had.

BILL. Pirate Willie's!

AMELIA. What?

BILL. That's the name of the place!

AMELIA. What place?

BILL. With the glowing drinks! Well not glowing, but bright yellow, bright green –

AMELIA. Oh my god…

BILL. Those horrible day-glo sugary drinks. That we used to get.

AMELIA. Oh my god, was it actually called Pirate Willie's?

BILL. I must drive past it every day.

AMELIA. Why did we drink those?

BILL. 'Cause we weren't thinking about what we were drinking. Come on.

AMELIA. What?

BILL. Come on. We're going right now.

AMELIA. I'm wearing a robe.

BILL. And I have sex hair. Come on.

AMELIA. They won't even let me in!

BILL. Sweetie, "Pirate Willie's" will let you in.

AMELIA. We're seriously doing this?

BILL. We're gonna get hammered on the grossest beverages in Miami. In or out?

>   (**AMELIA** *kisses him.*)

AMELIA. Let me put on some shoes.

>   (*She exits up the stairs.* **BILL** *pulls out his cell phone and makes a call.*)

BILL. Wait ten minutes. Then start bringing stuff in.

Ten

(Day. **BILL** *and* **VALERIE** *assemble a machine at the living room table.* **ABBIE** *is on the couch, wrapped in a blanket, watching a movie on a laptop.* **CONOR** *hovers near him.* **RAF** *watches* **CONOR**. **VALERIE** *suddenly stops assembling the device, puts down what she's working on, and checks her phone. She looks up to see* **BILL** *watching her.)*

VALERIE. I mean…if she's not there now she's missed it.

BILL. Val: in what world, in *what world*, would I blame you?

VALERIE. I need to focus.

(She returns to the device. **BELINDA** *enters with a ginger ale.)*

BELINDA. Hey Abbie.

ABBIE. *(taking it from her)* Thanks.

*(**CONOR** *moves a little closer, looking at the label on the can.* **ABBIE** *notices.)*

Conor. I'm okay. It's just a cold.

RAF. What's his problem?

BILL. Change in the routine. He knows Abbie should be in school right now.

ABBIE. He can tell I'm sick.

BILL. Well, he can tell something's different than usual.

ABBIE. He can tell I'm sick.

RAF. He's driving me fucking nuts.

BELINDA. *(to* **BILL***)* I also got the sat photos, you want 'em?

BILL. Please.

*(**BELINDA** *gets them out.)*

RAF. *(to* **CONOR***)* You wanna sit down or something?

BILL. *(to* **RAF***)* Do you need to take a walk?

RAF. Why don't you ever sit down?

BILL. Hey: take a walk.

RAF. Yeah, I'll take a walk, that's a good idea. Maybe down to the Wine and Liquor?

BILL. I mean, do it while you can.

> (RAF *exits out the front door.* BILL *studies the photos from* BELINDA.)

Okay, I'm looking at...

BELINDA. Numerical order, Everglades to Okavango.

BILL. Wow.

BELINDA. Right?

BILL. These are since...

BELINDA. Friday. Not even a week.

BILL. *(to* VALERIE*)* Do you see this?

VALERIE. *(studying the photos)* They're so...healthy.

BELINDA. Totally, it's like seeing a kid who grew two feet since the last time you saw them.

VALERIE. It's gonna be so fast.

> (ABBIE *has quietly removed one earbud and is listening.*)

BILL. What's the transmission window?

VALERIE. Which one?

BILL. Sorry, not for the pheromones, the first one.

VALERIE. If nobody spots us and shuts it down, thirty-five seconds.

BILL. So we should assume ten.

VALERIE. The briefer the message, the better. Shit! *(She puts down what she's working on.)*

BILL. Call her.

VALERIE. I've called her.

BILL. Call her again. 'Cause this is ridiculous.

> (VALERIE *grabs her phone and calls a number while walking into the kitchen.*)

Boy, this is some crew today, huh? Sick, sad, in withdrawal, *(to* CONOR*)* whatever you're doing...

BELINDA. I just want it done. It's waiting that's fucking me up.

ABBIE. *(pulling earbuds out)* Want what done?

> (**BELINDA** *looks at* **BILL**, *who thinks fast.*)

BILL. Hey Abbie, can I get a consult?

ABBIE. A consult on what?

BILL. I need an expert.

ABBIE. Um…do I need astronaut training, or…?

BILL. No no no, comic book training.

ABBIE. I think you have to finish at least one comic book before you can be an expert.

BILL. Forget that, you're an expert.

ABBIE. Okay, I'm an expert. Ask me anything.

BILL. Let's say, just for fun, let's say your characters, your insectoid, remind me…?

ABBIE. The Honeycomb.

> (*Over the following,* **CONOR** *quietly goes into the kitchen.*)

BILL. The Honeycomb, right. Let's say the Honeycomb was coming to Earth.

ABBIE. That's not what the story's about.

BILL. That's fine, I'm just saying what if they did?

ABBIE. Like, to explore?

BILL. Sure, whatever reason.

ABBIE. That would be funny. People would…

BILL. People would what?

ABBIE. If giant insects came out of the sky? People would lose their shit! Sorry. People would have an adverse reaction.

BILL. People would lose their shit.

ABBIE. How is this helping with your swamp farming?

BILL. We've got sites all over the world, diplomacy's a big part of what we do.

ABBIE. Okay, how is this helping with diplomacy?

BILL. What if the Honeycomb could send a message ahead, to let people know they're coming?

ABBIE. What message?

> *(**VALERIE** enters from the kitchen.)*

BILL. I'm asking you. They're your insects. How would they put it?

ABBIE. They don't speak English.

BILL. Let's say they can translate, it's not important.

ABBIE. You mean, "Don't lose your shit, we won't hurt you?"

BILL. But could they really promise that? If we attacked them they'd fight back, right?

ABBIE. Definitely.

BILL. So that's what I need. I need a message from the Honeycomb to the human race, telling us not to lose our shit and not attack them and everything will be fine, and I need it to fit into five seconds.

ABBIE. Five seconds?

BILL. One Mississippi, two Mississippi –

ABBIE. Why do you need it in five seconds?

BILL. It's a challenge. No school today, so that's your homework.

> *(**CONOR** enters with a can of ginger ale. He's trembling.)*

ABBIE. Or you'll give me an F?

BILL. Or I'll kick your ass.

ABBIE. On it. *(He rises to go upstairs.)*

BILL. Well you can do it here.

ABBIE. No, I need quiet if I'm –

CONOR. Abbie.

> *(They all turn to look at him. He holds out the soda can.)*

Abbie.

ABBIE. Oh… Thank you, Conor. Are you…

(*He puts down the can from* **CONOR** *and takes* **CONOR**'s *hand.* **VALERIE** *enters from the kitchen.*)

BILL. Is he all right?

ABBIE. I think it's the can. He didn't know it would be that cold.

BILL. (*to* **VALERIE**) Tell me.

VALERIE. She's…

BELINDA. You got her on the phone?

VALERIE. Bill, she won't make it without me.

ABBIE. Thank you, Conor. Seriously. (*He takes the ginger ale and goes upstairs.*)

BELINDA. What did she say?

VALERIE. It's so fucking unfair.

BILL. It's family. Family's unfair.

BELINDA. She missed it?

VALERIE. She got all the way to the airport and then didn't get on the plane. She said she couldn't face it. Not the flying, she couldn't face being in the plane with all those people.

BILL. Val –

VALERIE. It's so unfair of her to put me in this position!

BILL. Yeah but now –

VALERIE. My whole life, she falls apart and I swoop in. What if I wanted to fall apart? That sounds good. When can I try it?

BELINDA. I'd kinda like to see that.

(**VALERIE** *smiles.*)

No, do it right now real quick. Fall apart.

VALERIE. Those three years on the *Celeste*, with you guys, when she couldn't call me? That was as happy as I get.

BILL. Start searching flights.

VALERIE. No, fuck her.

BILL. Val: you've already decided.

VALERIE. Fuck that and fuck her!

(The doorbell rings.)

Are you expecting anyone?

*(**BILL** indicates no. **VALERIE** goes to the window.)*

It's Kip.

BILL. Are you kidding me?

VALERIE. Not so loud.

BILL. At this moment, at *this* moment, I have to focus on that obsequious –

VALERIE. Is this door soundproofed? All our cars are in the driveway.

BILL. *(to **BELINDA**)* Give me some papers.

BELINDA. Which ones?

BILL. Any papers.

*(**BELINDA** hands **BILL** some papers and he sits down and starts looking at them.)*

Okay.

*(**VALERIE** opens the door to reveal **KIP**.)*

VALERIE. Hi Kip!

KIP. Listen, I'm sorry, I'm sorry, I know how inappropriate this is –

BILL. Is that Kip? Holy shit, Kip? Get your ass in here!

*(As **KIP** enters, **BILL** hugs him.)*

KIP. Bill, this is your home, I want you to know I would never intrude on your home –

BILL. You know what this is? This is a happy ending to a shitty day. If you ever need to turn around a totally shitty day, nothing that beats the unexpected appearance of an old friend.

KIP. Bill, you have to understand, they're going to freeze my accounts.

BILL. I'm sorry?

KIP. They can do that, if they suspect I'm funding criminal activity –

BILL. Wait wait wait Kip, you've got to catch me up, here.

KIP. You told me you took care of this!

BILL. Who are you talking about, who said this?

KIP. I've been waiting at your office – please – I wouldn't have come to your home, but your people at the office, they keep putting me off – Bill, I put forty million dollars into this!

BILL. Kip, look –

KIP. Shit, is that him? Is that Conor?

BILL. Kip: *look at me.* Look at my face. I'm still the same guy. Whatever the problem is, I know we can solve it.

KIP. They're everywhere I go. They're at my office, they're at my club –

BILL. Again, Kip, I'm gonna need to know who "they" are.

KIP. Men. In suits. It seems like different guys every time.

> (**BILL** *looks over* **KIP'S** *shoulder at* **VALERIE**, *who is already getting out her phone and pretending she has a call.*)

VALERIE. Sorry, I have to get this. *(She exits into the kitchen.)*

BILL. Hey, I know that would scare me.

KIP. This is what I've been trying to tell you! They're asking about the investments, they're asking about the sites – but you haven't let me visit the sites!

BILL. You know what, we were gonna set that up for the beginning of next week – Belinda, have we set a time for that yet?

BELINDA. Yes sir, first thing Monday we can take Kip to the Everglades site, or really any of them – we can charter a plane –

BILL. That's great news, I've been really hoping to make that happen for a while –

KIP. They're saying you dismissed everyone working on the sites. Months ago.

BILL. Who now?

KIP. The farmers, the ecologists, *months ago.*

BILL. Well of course, past a certain point the crop is self-sustaining – wasn't that in the presentation?

BELINDA. I'm sure it was.

KIP. They asked me about Tom Wiley. *(beat)*

BILL. What about Tom Wiley?

KIP. They asked me what I know about his death.

BILL. Tom Wiley.

KIP. And about Conor, too, what do I know about his accident, what do I know –

BILL. Well huh, this is kinda funny, apparently these men in suits didn't hear about a NASA inquiry on the public record finding absolutely no evidence –

KIP. And the satellites.

BILL. What satellites?

KIP. They're saying my money's being used – they're asking what I know about unauthorized use of satellites – but that's crazy, right? What do satellites have to do with anything?

> (**BILL** *looks at* **BELINDA**, *who sidles quietly into the kitchen after* **VALERIE**. *Over the following,* **CONOR** *sees the satellite photos that* **BELINDA** *brought in. He walks to the table for a closer look, and then picks them up.)*

BILL. Okay, let me just say straight out of the gate: we're going to be fine.

KIP. They're telling me I'm funding, I don't know, maybe terrorism, or treason –

BILL. Terrorism?

KIP. Or treason, different guys say different things.

BILL. We're growing vegetables here.

KIP. They're saying they'll freeze everything. That I'll have nothing. That if I want breakfast I'll have to borrow five dollars from my ex-wife.

BILL. Well, they sound like some real tough guys, don't they?

KIP. Bill, you *know*, you know I admire you more than anyone I can think of – I mean –

BILL. Kip, you know we have enemies, right? I hope I've never tried to pretend that's not true.

KIP. Yeah, I guess, I mean...

BILL. When you see someone like me, espousing radical change in environmental policy, in economic policy, you've got to know I'm threatening the livelihood of some very powerful people. It's actually amazing this hasn't happened before.

> (VALERIE *and* BELINDA *re-enter.* BILL *exchanges looks with them.*)

KIP. I know, Bill, I mean, I totally hear that, it's just – If I could just see one of the sites, if I could, I could take my cell phone, take some pictures of the crop –

BILL. We're doing that Monday. Isn't that the plan? Didn't we just say Monday?

CONOR. When is dinner?

KIP. Or, you know, now, even.

BILL. Boy, *now?* I gotta tell you, Kip –

KIP. I know you're a busy man.

VALERIE. Bill, we're set for that phone conference in ten minutes –

BILL. I mean, *I'd* love to, just –

KIP. The Everglades site is less than an hour away, Bill, please. Just so I can see it with my own eyes. We can go right after your phone conference, I can wait.

CONOR. When is dinner?

BILL. Kip, it'll be Monday before you know it. We'll take the jeep, put the top down –

KIP. I can't wait through the weekend, Bill, I can't sleep.

CONOR. When is dinner?

BILL. *(to* CONOR*)* Okay, buddy, I hear you, just give me a minute.

KIP. Is he hungry, or –

(**CONOR** *brandishes the photographs.*)

CONOR. Bill! When is dinner!

KIP. Jesus.

BELINDA. Hey, Conor, you wanna go for a walk with me –

> (*She touches him.* **CONOR** *shrieks and jerks away from her.*)

Shit!

CONOR. (*shaking the drawing at* **BILL**) When is dinner! Bill!

VALERIE. (*approaching but not touching him*) Dinner is soon, Conor. Okay? Dinner is soon. Dinner is soon.

KIP. Look, I can – I can even wait in my car.

CONOR. (*still holding up the photos*) Bill.

BILL. Kip let me make you a proposition. Obviously I need to take care of my friend here.

KIP. I'm saying, I can wait, we can go in an hour –

BILL. But let me make you this proposition. If you let me take care of my friend right now, I can promise you that tomorrow morning, I will show you the site and I will make the men in the suits stop bothering you.

KIP. I think if I could just show them pictures of –

CONOR. Bill.

VALERIE. Dinner is soon, Conor.

BILL. They're not the only ones with strings to pull. I'm saying, give me until tomorrow, and I promise you, these people will be off your back forever.

KIP. By tomorrow? Like twenty-four hours.

BILL. Not even. By the *morning*.

KIP. And you'll show me the Everglades site.

BILL. First thing tomorrow. As early as you feel like getting up. You give me tonight, and I swear to you, tomorrow you're gonna see zero men in suits, and as much swamp as you could possibly desire.

> (*beat*)

KIP. I'm sorry, Bill.

BILL. There's nothing to be sorry for.

KIP. These guys have me jammed up, I'm not sleeping –

BILL. Don't explain, don't apologize, you're part of this team. We stick together.

BELINDA. Lemme walk you to your car, Kip.

KIP. Bill, I'm sorry, I'm tired, you know, I'm jumping at the littlest sounds –

BILL. Well I'm no doctor, but it sounds like a nap is in order.

KIP. Jesus. Imagine that. A nap.

BILL. How's this, Kip: see you tomorrow, right here, 8 a.m., I'll bring the beer.

KIP. Sounds amazing.

(BELINDA's walking him out.)

BELINDA. I haven't seen your car, you have one of those fancy hybrids, right?

(She exits with KIP.)

VALERIE. My contact doesn't know much.

CONOR. Bill.

BILL. Right with you, buddy.

VALERIE. It's FBI. They got a tip a week days ago.

BILL. Before the PI came in here.

VALERIE. I guess she really did call for backup. They were already looking at us. They just stepped it up.

BILL. Doesn't matter now.

CONOR. Bill! When is dinner?

VALERIE. What has gotten into him?

BILL. Look what he's holding.

VALERIE. The sat photos.

BILL. The vegetation, the egg sacs, the Honeycomb. He recognizes all of it.

CONOR. When is dinner?

VALERIE. But Conor didn't see any of that, he was already down before they showed us the sample.

BILL. Exactly.

> *(They look at* **CONOR.** *)*

I said we'd know when he told us.

CONOR. Bill, when is dinner?

> (**ABBIE** *appears at the top of the stairs with a paper.*
> *He stops and holds still. No one notices him.)*

BILL. What are you asking? Yes, they're what you think they are. Is that what it is?

> (**BELINDA** *re-enters over the following.)*

VALERIE. What if he means…?

BILL. What?

VALERIE. Conor – Ambassador – the ones who were with you? When we found you? They died.

CONOR. When is dinner?

VALERIE. You understand, died?

CONOR. *(despondent)* Died?

BILL. I'm so sorry.

VALERIE. But they're not gone. You know that, right?

BILL. That's right, they're not gone. Everything they knew, all their memories, everything they've ever seen, it's all sleeping in the Honeycomb.

CONOR. Bill.

BILL. The Honeycomb is asleep, but it's not dead. *Not dead.*

CONOR. Nnnnot dead.

BILL. *Not dead.* It's waking up. You know "tomorrow"? It's waking up tomorrow.

BELINDA. Tomorrow?

BILL. *(lower, to* **BELINDA***)* Tonight. They're on to us. *(to* **VALERIE***)* Get online. There's flights to LA every night. It'll be a thousand dollars. Get it anyway.

VALERIE. Might as well. Can't spend it tomorrow. Oh Jesus.

> (**BILL** *holds her.)*

BILL. I built this whole thing around my family. How could I ask you to do less?

VALERIE. What about the transmitter?

BELINDA. We'll finish the transmitter.

VALERIE. You'll mess it up.

BELINDA. *(to* BILL*)* Can you believe this shit?

BILL. We can't put it out 'til dark anyway. I have neighbors. Go find a flight.

> *(As* VALERIE *goes to her computer, they all notice* ABBIE.*)*

Hey.

Hey kiddo.

ABBIE. I wrote the thing.

CONOR. *(showing the photographs)* Abbie.

BILL. Great, let's see – actually, first, can you grab your cell phone and bring that too?

ABBIE. My cell phone?

BILL. Yeah, bring me your cell phone and bring me what you wrote. I'll show you what I mean.

CONOR. Abbie. Dinner is soon.

> *(sounds of a car pulling up outside)*

ABBIE. That's great, Conor. What'cha got there?

BELINDA. Amelia's pulling up.

BILL. Is Ronnie with her?

BELINDA. Yeah.

ABBIE. Dad, what's happening tomorrow?

BILL. Grab your cell phone and I'll show you.

> *(*ABBIE *exits up the stairs. To* BELINDA*.)*

Cut the lines. Now.

BELINDA. Yep.

> *(She exits through the kitchen.* AMELIA *enters with drug store purchases.)*

AMELIA. Oh – hi Valerie. That's…wow, that's quite a thing. *(calling out)* Ronnie! Come on!

VALERIE. Sorry it's such a mess, Amelia.

AMELIA. Well, I'm the one who invited you.

BILL. Hey Milly, can I see your phone?

AMELIA. What?

BILL. Your cell phone, can I – actually, let me help you with that. *(He takes the bags from her hands and sets them on the couch.)* Can I see your cell phone?

AMELIA. *(meaning the bags)* Okay, but that's not where I was going to put those.

BILL. Just real quick.

AMELIA. *(getting out her phone)* What, is yours not working?

> *(**BILL** takes it from her hand.)*

BILL. Thanks, sorry sweetheart.

VALERIE. Can I help you with those bags?

AMELIA. No, I'm fine.

> *(She carries the bags to the kitchen. **RONNIE** enters through the front door.)*

RONNIE. Whoa. What happened here?

BILL. Come on in, Ron.

RONNIE. I hope that thing plays music.

BILL. Can I see your cell phone?

RONNIE. What?

BILL. Can I just look at your cell phone?

RONNIE. Why?

> *(**AMELIA** comes out of the kitchen.)*

AMELIA. Bill? Are our phones not working?

BILL. They're not working?

AMELIA. The landline's dead. Are you done with my cell?

BILL. Do you need to make a call right now?

AMELIA. Do I *need* to?

(*ABBIE comes down the stairs with his cell phone and a paper.*)

ABBIE. Hi Mom.

AMELIA. Oh – Abbie. Are you feeling better sweetie?

ABBIE. I think so. I still feel a little hot. (*to* BILL) Here's my phone. What were you gonna show me? (*BILL takes ABBIE's phone.*)

BILL. Let me get your phone, Ronnie.

RONNIE. That's okay.

BILL. I'm sorry?

RONNIE. Looks like you've already got two, so...

BILL. I need to see yours.

(*RAF enters behind* RONNIE.)

RONNIE. But you've got two. Plus your own. That's three.

AMELIA. Bill?

ABBIE. I think he's going to show us something – is it like a trick?

BILL. Okay, Ronnie, there's a time and a place. But it's not now.

RONNIE. I'm gonna keep my phone.

BILL. I know we're buds, I know we're pals, and most of the time that's fine, but when it comes down to it, I'm the father.

AMELIA. Bill, what's going on?

BILL. And you're the child. And you do what I say.

(*RONNIE turns around.* RAF's *behind her, closing the front door and standing in front of it.*)

RONNIE. I'm not giving you my phone.

AMELIA. Bill, could I talk to you in the kitchen, please?

RONNIE. It's my phone. You can't have it.

BILL. It's okay if you wanna cry.

RONNIE. I'm not crying.

(*BELINDA enters.*)

BILL. I sound a little weird right now. Maybe I sound a little different. That's probably a little scary.

RONNIE. I'm not crying.

BILL. I'm not saying you are, I'm saying it's okay if you want to.

AMELIA. Bill!

RONNIE. You can't have my phone!

BILL. It's fun to play rebel. It's a fun game. But we're not playing games now. That's what you hear in my voice, that the game is over. That's what's making you feel like crying.

RONNIE. Why are you saying that, I'm not crying!

BILL. I'm saying you *can*. It's nothing to be ashamed of.

AMELIA. Bill that's *enough*.

> (*She starts to cross the room.* **VALERIE** *rises sharply to her feet, intercepting her...* **AMELIA,** *startled, stops and looks at her.*)

BILL. *(to* **RONNIE***)* You're strong and brave. You'll always be strong and brave. Just 'cause you cry doesn't take that away.

> (**RONNIE** *is crying. She's furious.* **BILL** *gently takes her bag, opens it, and pulls out her cell phone.*)

Abbie?

ABBIE. What?

BILL. What did you come up with?

ABBIE. What's happening, Dad?

BILL. What did you write down?

ABBIE. I could barely fit anything in five seconds. I had to cut out so much.

BILL. So what was left?

ABBIE. "If you don't hurt us, we won't hurt you."

BILL. Perfect.

Eleven

(**RAF**, *holding* **LYNN**'s *gun, watches out the front window. Then goes to the sofa, sets the gun down, and sits.* **RONNIE** *appears on the stairs, watching him.* **RAF** *starts to make a call, then stops.*)

RONNIE. Why didn't you call?

RAF. Who?

RONNIE. *(going to the window)* Whoever you decided not to call.

RAF. Mind your business. *(beat)* Tonight I said goodbye to one of my best friends forever.

RONNIE. And that made you want to call somebody?

RAF. Do you ever fucking let up? *(beat)* Glad we didn't go through with it, would've been like fucking your dad.

RONNIE. Bonershrinker. *(indicating outside)* Who's that for, anyway?

RAF. What?

RONNIE. That hole my Dad's digging. Who's it for?

RAF. You're ridiculous.

RONNIE. Why *didn't* we go through with it?

RAF. You don't remember kicking me out?

RONNIE. What if I hadn't?

RAF. What, tiptoed past your parents' bedroom?

RONNIE. *(sitting by him on the couch)* Or wherever.

RAF. Two types of girls go for me: stupid ones who think they can fix me, and smart ones who feel like doing something stupid.

RONNIE. Stupid can be fun.

RAF. All right, okay.

RONNIE. I keep thinking, what if I hadn't kicked you out?

RAF. Yeah?

RONNIE. Yeah. I've been thinking about it a lot.

(She leans into RAF and kisses him. He sort of kisses back. She leans into him, pushing him back on the couch. As she gets more on top of him, she reaches her hand over to the gun. RAF grabs her wrist.)

RONNIE. Hey – hey! Let go of me!

(RAF takes the gun out of her hand, releases her.)

RAF. Can I give you a hint? Honey-trap's not your thing.

(Over the following, RONNIE quietly takes his cell phone off the table and hides it.)

I don't know what it is. Any other girl, I would've let that run it's course, 'cause at this point, why not?

RONNIE. What is "this point"?

RAF. Damn, look at that, already bounced back. Are you ever *not* trying something? What were you gonna do? Shoot your way out?

RONNIE. Maybe.

RAF. Man, I love this. I can't even tell you. It's ultimate cosmic fuck-you to Bill Cooke to have a kid like you. Except…shit, he probably used to be just the same. I better do my part digging before your old man pulls something.

RONNIE. Aren't you supposed to be guarding the door?

RAF. Run if you want. Just remember: Don't hurt them and they won't hurt you.

(RAF leaves. RONNIE checks the window to watch him go, then pulls out his cell phone, checks that it works. She goes thundering up the stairs.)

RONNIE. *(offstage)* MOM!! MOM, WAKE UP ABBIE!

(She comes back down the stairs, runs for the window. She pulls out the phone, gets to the keypad screen, thinks. AMELIA comes downstairs.)

AMELIA. Ronnie what hell is going on?

RONNIE. Where's Abbie? I said we need Abbie!

AMELIA. Abbie's asleep, what are you –?

RONNIE. Well go get him!

AMELIA. Excuse me?

RONNIE. *(indicating out the window)* They could come back any minute!

AMELIA. *(looking out window)* Is that an antenna?

RONNIE. Whatever it is, they're almost finished with it!

> (**ABBIE** *appears on the stairs in a t-shirt and pajama pants.*)

ABBIE. Mom?

RONNIE. Put some clothes on, Jesus, we might have to leave any second!

ABBIE. Why?

AMELIA. Leave?

RONNIE. *(to* **ABBIE***)* At least put some shoes on! *(to* **AMELIA***)* See, here's the thing: if we tell the cops Dad's beating me, they'll send a car, right?

AMELIA. *What?*

RONNIE. Except, Raf said…

AMELIA. Jesus, Ronnie – no one's telling anybody anything until we think a minute. Now I'm going to make some coffee, and when your father comes back –

RONNIE. *You're gonna make some coffee?*

AMELIA. All right, that is absolutely *it.* I understand this is a strange situation –

RONNIE. Strange?

AMELIA. But you're just using it as license to run around and scream your head off.

RONNIE. He took all our phones! He's building some crazy thing on the lawn!

ABBIE. Guys, please stop!

AMELIA. *And it's the best thing that's ever happened to you!* It's the best excuse you've ever had!

RONNIE. Mom!

AMELIA. I'm not some kind of placid fool because I don't want to run out of our home in the middle of the night to – where exactly? – when we don't even know what's happening.

> (**CONOR** *appears on the stairs. He has the photos with him.*)

RONNIE. What would it take for you to go against him ever?

AMELIA. All right, I've been courteous, but now I'm just gonna be Mom and tell you to shut up.

RONNIE. Wow, it sounds a lot better coming from him.

AMELIA. Why can't you *stop*?

ABBIE. Guys, please, I can't take it!

CONOR. Abbie.

> (**ABBIE** *goes to* **CONOR** *and embraces him.* **CONOR** *stiffens.*)

AMELIA. Abbie – baby – you can't just touch him like that, he's gonna...

> (**CONOR** *relaxes. He puts the arm not holding the photos around* **ABBIE.**)

Oh my God.

CONOR. Abbie home.

RONNIE. "I just said goodbye to one of my best friends forever." That's what Raf just told me.

AMELIA. Right, Valerie, she had to –

CONOR. *(showing sat photos)* Abbie, dinner is soon.

RONNIE. But why "forever"? Why wouldn't they see each other again *forever*?

ABBIE. *(to* **CONOR***)* I'm sorry, I don't understand.

AMELIA. There's any number of reasons a person might say –

RONNIE. Right, and there's any number of reasons someone might take away his family's phones, or someone might be building a freaky antenna in the front yard with his friends all night? What are some of these reasons?

AMELIA. *(approaching* **RONNIE***)* Sweetheart…

RONNIE. I need you. *(beat)*

AMELIA. All right. Tell me, without the hysteria, what you think we should do.

RONNIE. If we tell the police they'll just hide what they're doing and start again later. You have to get him to tell us what he's doing. He won't tell me. He'll tell you.

> *(***BILL***, ***BELINDA***, and* ***RAF*** *enter through the front door.* ***BELINDA*** *carries a device, which she sets up over the following.)*

BILL. Or you can just ask.

CONOR. *(approaching him with the pictures)* Bill. Bill.

BILL. You guys are up early.

AMELIA. Well, Bill, why do you think that is?

CONOR. When is dinner?

BILL. Dinner is soon, buddy.

ABBIE. Dad, what are those pictures of?

AMELIA. Maybe it's time for Raf and Belinda to go home now.

ABBIE. I've never seen him this excited like ever.

BILL. *(looking at* **AMELIA***)* Well, what if you hadn't seen me or your mom or Ronnie in many years, and then somebody showed you a picture of us?

AMELIA. Raf? Belinda? I'm going to ask –

BILL. He's happy to see his family.

> *(***BELINDA*** *gets a text on her phone.)*

Tell me.

BELINDA. She's landed. They're taking her to her rental car now.

RAF. Jesus.

ABBIE. *(looking at* **CONOR***)* His family?

BILL. *(to* **BELINDA***)* Get it working.

RONNIE. How did you know to come in? How did you know we were leaving?

BILL. *(removing an earpiece from his ear)* Ask your mother. She's the one who hired a private detective to hide a listening device in this room. *(to* **RONNIE***)* Ask me. Ask me anything you want to know.

AMELIA. Where is she now?

BILL. She's fine. She's just not working for you anymore.

AMELIA. All right, we're leaving.

BILL. Milly.

AMELIA. Abbie. Change into some clothes. We're leaving.

ABBIE. Dad?

BILL. It's okay, kiddo.

AMELIA. Go upstairs, put some clothes on, and come right back.

CONOR. *(showing the pictures again)* Abbie.

BILL. Why don't you guys go back to bed and we'll talk in a couple hours?

AMELIA. How are you going to stop us?

BILL. What?

AMELIA. Are you gonna tie us up? Abbie, go get dressed.

CONOR. Abbie home.

BILL. Tie you – do you know how crazy you sound?

RONNIE. Or Raf has a gun. Are you gonna shoot us if we try to leave?

BILL. Jesus, Raf, you still have that?

RAF. I don't know, what if –?

BILL. You can't have that here when it happens!

RONNIE. When what happens?

AMELIA. We're going.

ABBIE. *(meaning the photos)* I wanna know what this is.

BILL. *(to* **AMELIA***)* You can't. It's not safe.

AMELIA. Out there, it's not safe? *That's* where it's not safe?

RAF. He's right, Amelia.

AMELIA. Well, Raf, I don't think I care about your opinion.

RAF. It's not an opinion.

AMELIA. Then you'd better tell us what's happening, because if you don't, I'm taking our children and walking out that door right now, out where it's *not safe.*

BILL. You don't understand, *you can't leave.*

RONNIE. *(pulling out* **RAF***'s phone)* Sure we can.

BELINDA. What the fuck?

RAF. Oh shit.

BELINDA. Is that your fucking phone?

RONNIE. Let's see, "nine," "one"...

BILL. Ronnie don't!

BELINDA. Fucking stop her!

RONNIE. "One." And then if I hit "Send"...

BILL. Don't!

BELINDA. They'll send cops with guns! We can't have cops with guns here when it happens!

AMELIA. *When what happens?*

BILL. All right, look, *look!*

> *(He frantically unfolds a paper from his pocket, shows it to* **RONNIE.***)*

Remember this? Remember Abbie drawing this?

CONOR. *(pointing at the photos and the drawing)* Abbie! Abbie!

BILL. That's right, buddy.

> *(He takes a sat photo, shows it and the drawing to* **RONNIE.***)*

Okay, this? Right here? This is a satellite photo of the Chinampas preserve in the Everglades. This is an egg sac containing something like five million eggs. And there's three of these in every Chinampas swamp-farming preserve in the world. Now in a few minutes we're gonna get a phone call from Valerie saying she's safely reached her sister's house, and when we do, we're gonna flip that switch over there, which will release natal pheromones at every one of the sites in the world, and when those eggs hatch – *(He holds up* **ABBIE***'s drawing.)* – this is what's going to come out.

RAF. *(looking at the drawing)* Shit, that looks just like them.

BILL. Now they won't hurt anyone who doesn't hurt them. But if there are men with guns at this house shooting at them? It will be really, really bad. So sweetheart, Ronnie, I promise you: you really want to put that phone down.

AMELIA. *(looking around at the astronauts)* You're not joking. None of you are joking.

BELINDA. You don't have to believe us. You can just wait.

BILL. Their planet's gone dry, they can't live on it anymore. They were looking for a new one when they crash-landed on Mars. Where we found them.

ABBIE. The Honeycomb's real.

AMELIA. Abbie, hold on.

BILL. *(to AMELIA)* Remember? "Rapidly relocate choice personnel?" But I didn't tell you what they said next.

BELINDA. Those fucking people.

RAF. You can picture it, right? Us all sitting around that room, after like *months* of briefings on fossil fuel depletion, uh, what, population spikes –

BELINDA. Mass extinctions, whole species: birds, amphibians, insects, just quietly *gone.*

RAF. *(to BILL)* How did he put it?

BILL. *(to AMELIA)* He looked around at our faces, like six ghosts, and he said: "Of course *your* families would be included in any relocation. Of course *your* families would be included." And then stuffed us in a steel box to think about *that* for fourteen months. By the time the he – *(indicating CONOR)* – told us, "You're dying, we're dying, maybe we can help each other," there were no six people in the human race more ready to listen.

BELINDA. Five people.

BILL. Right.

RONNIE. Meaning one of you wasn't ready to listen.

BILL. Okay, good, sweetheart, and which one was that?

RONNIE. The one who didn't come back. Tom Wiley.

(a signal from the machine)

BELINDA. Shit – Bill – I've got signal. We're go to transmit the warning.

BILL. *(to* ABBIE*)* This is your big moment, kiddo. *(to* BELINDA*)* Read it back to me.

BELINDA. "If you don't hurt us, we won't hurt you."

BILL. *(to* RONNIE*)* That's what they told us on Mars. Tom Wiley was the only one who didn't listen. That's why you can't leave this house. And that's why you can't make that call. *(to* BELINDA*)* Do it.

> (BELINDA *operates the device.* RONNIE *slowly lowers the phone.)*

BELINDA. Sending now.

BILL. *(to* ABBIE*)* Those are your words, kiddo. Beaming out over broadcast lines all over the world. That's gonna save millions of lives today. Millions.

BELINDA. We gotta go through with it now, right? I *love* it!

RAF. Fuck, Val better call soon.

AMELIA. What do you mean, *he* said it?

BILL. Said what?

AMELIA. *(indicating* CONOR*)* "We're dying, maybe we can help each other."

BILL. Well, who do you think he is?

AMELIA. I'm sorry?

BILL. Who do you think he is? How do you think they told us?

AMELIA. These, I'm sorry, these *aliens* you met on Mars.

RONNIE. What, they speak English?

BELINDA. They don't speak anything. They're telepathic, they share a hive mind.

BILL. *(pointing to* CONOR*)* So they needed a translator.

ABBIE. Oh my god.

CONOR. Abbie. Ronnie. Amelia. Dinner is soon.

BILL. They would put a thought in his mind, and Conor would say it out loud. Everything they could offer our planet. How we could make it happen. How to hide the spores in our bodies, how to build environments where they could incubate and hatch. He lasted close to seventy-two hours.

AMELIA. "Lasted"?

BELINDA. We don't know what happened. Something went wrong.

BILL. What it looked like was the Ambassador died and Conor had a stroke.

ABBIE. *Of course!*

BILL. *(to* **ABBIE***)* Do you have it?

ABBIE. The Ambassador didn't die – Conor did! The Ambassador's brain got stuck inside Conor's body!

AMELIA. Abbie, get away from him.

ABBIE. He's not gonna hurt me, Mom!

> (**ABBIE** *takes the sat photos and the drawing and shows them to* **CONOR***.)*

This is you?

CONOR. Home, Abbie, Abbie, home.

ABBIE. This is you.

CONOR. Dinner is soon.

AMELIA. And you brought him back?

BILL. Not me. You. You brought him back.

AMELIA. I…

BILL. Think how scared he must have been: locked in a strange, soft body, looking through eyes, hearing through ears for the first time, surrounded by terror. You brought him out of that, you gave him his legs, his voice, a family, a *home.* That's you, Amelia Cooke: the first Ambassador of the human race.

ABBIE. *(to* **CONOR***)* Ambassador.

AMELIA. I don't believe you.

BILL. That's okay.

AMELIA. I don't believe any of this!

BILL. There'll be plenty of proof in a few minutes.

RONNIE. When they hatch.

BILL. That's right, sweetie.

RONNIE. And then what? They hatch and then what happens?

BELINDA. Five weeks to subdue and knock out the remaining generators. Then a year for terraform.

RONNIE. Terraform?

BILL. The first year will be hard. Total climate adjustment, it'll be a lot of work. But when we're done? We get our new lives.

BELINDA. I think about it all the time.

BILL. We'll work. We'll raise crops. We'll help build their nests. This neighborhood? It's gonna be our village. No electricity, no cars, the skies will clear, the stars will come out at night. The world won't belong to the strong and the greedy anymore. *(to* **ABBIE***)* Bullies, teachers, making your life a misery? Not anymore. Under the Honeycomb we're all the same. We'll take care of each other. And we'll always be together.

RONNIE. What if I don't want that to be my life?

BILL. Are you kidding? Nobody will, at first. As spoiled as we are? But give it some time, let that tranquility set in, *(to* **RONNIE***)* and that anger you've been running around with your whole life? *(to* **ABBIE***)* Those terrifying thoughts, those faces, crowding up your mind? That's all gonna drift away and leave you with perfect, quiet contentment. Won't that feel amazing?

RONNIE. No.

BILL. *(to* **AMELIA***)* Someone at some point has to say "I'm not just gonna take care of my little corner." That's what you do, Milly, and you do it beautifully, I've always said. But somebody has to come along who's *not* gonna put their own first or things never get better.

AMELIA. And the whole time you've been thinking all this… you never once brought it to me.

BILL. Because that's not you, Milly. I love you, but that's not you. You leave the house for groceries or when someone misses the bus.

RONNIE. Mom.

AMELIA. I just…

BILL. How many times did you watch me thinking in silence and not ask? Be honest. How many times did you hear me on the phone in the next room and choose *not* to listen?

AMELIA. I started listening.

BILL. And why was that? Why did you start listening?

RONNIE. Mom, we have to go now.

BILL. *(still on* **AMELIA***)* Go where? Go to who? Tell them what?

AMELIA. Stop.

RONNIE. Mom, we know, we have to go.

AMELIA. Stop.

BILL. And if they believe you, what? Have them take me away? Split up this family forever?

AMELIA. Stop it.

RONNIE. Mom.

BILL. Make the choice.

AMELIA. Stop it! I can't think while you're talking, stop it!

BILL. Think back, Milly: what made you start listening?

AMELIA. You were never home. I thought there was someone else. I thought you were leaving me.

BILL. Never.

AMELIA. First Ronnie, then Abbie, then you.

BILL. Never. *Never.* There's no one else. For me? There's never been anyone else.

(*Weeping,* **AMELIA** *rushes toward* **BILL.***)*

RONNIE. Mom!

AMELIA. *(to* RONNIE.*)* Why can't you ever *shut up?*

> *(She goes to* BILL, *who embraces her.* BELINDA*'s phone rings. Over the following,* RONNIE *sees* RAF*'s attention distracted.)*

BELINDA. Thank God. *(She answers.)* Yeah Val. Okay. And you're… Okay. Well then. *(Beat, listening.)* I love you too. We all love you. *(She hangs up.)* It's time.

BILL. Throw the switch.

> *(*RONNIE *suddenly lunges for the gun in* RAF*'s pants.)*

RAF. Hey!

RONNIE. *(pointing the gun at* BELINDA*)* Don't touch it!

BILL. Ronnie – all right – Ronnie –

AMELIA. Ronnie put it down!

CONOR. Abbie!

> *(*CONOR *pulls* ABBIE *back.* RONNIE *points the gun, one-handed, at* BELINDA.*)*

RONNIE. Don't touch it. Get away from it.

BILL. Ronnie put it down right now. You're gonna kill somebody.

BELINDA. Okay, kid, you're not gonna shoot me.

RONNIE. *(to* BELINDA*)* Let's find out.

CONOR. *(trying to explain why it's okay)* Ronnie, Ronnie, dinner is soon!

BELINDA. Bill, I'm just gonna flip it. She's not gonna shoot.

AMELIA. Ronnie, put it down!

BILL. Wait, wait, Belinda –

> *(*BELINDA *tries to throw the switch.* RONNIE *fires. Her wrist jerks with the impact of the shot.* BELINDA *cradles her elbow.)*

BELINDA. Shit!

BILL. What, what, are you hit?

BELINDA. If she could shoot straight I'd be fucking dead!

RAF. *(to* **RONNIE***)* You gotta hold it with both hands.

RONNIE. Next time I will.

BELINDA. Jesus!

AMELIA. Ronnie *put it down*! You're gonna hurt someone very badly.

(**BILL** *goes for the switch.*)

RONNIE. Hey – HEY! *(She points the gun at his chest.)* Stop!

BILL. *(edging closer to the switch)* All right, Ronnie? I'm sorry. Okay? I've been disrespecting you, and I'm sorry.

RONNIE. Stay away from it!

BILL. I've been treating you like a girl, but you're a woman. I was wrong, and I'm sorry.

RONNIE. If you touch it I'll kill you.

AMELIA. Ronnie please, I'm begging you –

RONNIE. Go to hell.

BILL. You're an adult. I'm an adult. We both know the difference between right and wrong. So what's gonna happen is, I'm gonna do the right thing, and you're gonna do the right thing. Okay? How does that sound?

(He reaches for the switch.)

RONNIE. Don't you do it.

RAF. *(calmly)* You know what, Bill? Look at her. She's not kidding. She's ready to kill you.

BILL. *(to* **RONNIE***)* This is for you! I did this all for you!

RONNIE. This is my life!

BILL. *You're gonna have your life! You're gonna have a beautiful life!*

(**ABBIE** *suddenly goes to the device, reaches for the switch.* **RONNIE** *points the gun at him, but can't fire.* **ABBIE** *throws the switch.*)

ABBIE. Okay? It's done! It's done! Okay? Now you can stop! Now you can put it down, and you can stop!

RONNIE. Abbie.

ABBIE. I wanna meet them. I wanna meet Conor's family. I want my brain to go quiet. I want to be free.

(*RAF gently takes the gun from* **RONNIE**.)

RAF. It's better like this. We fuck up every good thing we have. Trust me, I know. It's time to let somebody else drive.

AMELIA. Sweetheart.

(*She rushes to* **RONNIE** *and embraces her.* **RONNIE** *is stiff and still in her arms.* **BILL** *goes to* **BELINDA**.)

BILL. Let me see.

CONOR. (*running to a window*) Abbie, Abbie, Abbie!

ABBIE. What? You hear something? (**CONOR** *is checking different windows.*)

AMELIA. (*to* **RONNIE**) Are you all right?

BILL. (*looking at* **BELINDA**'s *arm*) Shit, I don't know, maybe there's still time…

BELINDA. As close as the Everglades is? They'll be here any minute.

BILL. I'm sorry.

BELINDA. I signed up for it.

RAF. (*joining* **ABBIE** *and* **CONOR** *at the windows*) Anything good, guys? (*He looks.*) Yeah. That's them.

(*In the distance, a buzzing begins. As it gets closer it's intermingled with chirping sounds.*)

AMELIA. What is that?

BILL. Already?

CONOR. Dinner is soon! Dinner is soon! Abbie!

ABBIE. I see them!

AMELIA. Oh my God, what is that?

(*Suddenly the sound of a flying object colliding with the house. Then another. We hear the skittering of insect legs running around on the roof.*)

What *is* that?

BILL. They won't hurt us.

> *(The dawn light outside is darkening. The buzzing and chirping is getting louder.)*

CONOR. Abbie! Abbie!

ABBIE. I see them!

CONOR. Home!

AMELIA. They're monsters! They're as big as dogs!

BELINDA. Then they're still growing.

BILL. They won't hurt you, sweetheart.

RAF. You know what? I'm going outside. Say hello.

BILL. Yeah?

RAF. In for a penny, in for a pound.

BELINDA. Hey. Asshole.

> *(RAF helps BELINDA to her feet and supports her as they go to the door.)*

AMELIA. No, NO, DON'T!

> *(RAF opens the door. The buzzing is momentarily much louder as he and BELINDA exit, then a bit quieter as he closes the door behind him. A crackle as the power goes out.)*

Oh my God. Oh my God.

BILL. You have to be strong now. You have to be strong for our children.

AMELIA. I can't.

> *(By now it's much darker, and we can hear insect legs on all sides of the house, skittering up and down the walls.)*

BILL. You can.

> *(RONNIE, a little away from the others, watches the two couples: BILL and AMELIA, ABBIE and CONOR. She goes to the stairs.)*

AMELIA. Ronnie?

(**RONNIE** *gives no sign of hearing as she ascends the stairs.*)

Ronnie!

BILL. Let her go. Let her go for now.

AMELIA. *Ronnie!*

BILL. Let her go.

(**RONNIE** *exits up the stairs.* **ABBIE** *and* **CONOR** *look out the window.*)

CONOR. Abbie.

ABBIE. They're perfect. They're perfect. It's like we drew them and they came to life.

CONOR. Abbie! Not dead! Not dead! Home!

(Lights down.)

The Play is Over

CPSIA information can be obtained
at www.ICGtesting.com
Printed in the USA
LVHW051809210119
604682LV00017B/677/P